A Knight to Remember

A Merriweather Sisters Time Travel Novel
Book 1

Cynthia Luhrs

This book is a work of fiction. Names, characters, places, and incidents either are products of the author's imagination or are used fictitiously.

A Knight to Remember, A Merriweather Sisters Time Travel Novel

Copyright © 2015 by Cynthia Luhrs

Acknowledgments

Thanks to my fabulous editor, Arran at Editing720 and Kendra at Typos Be Gone.

To my mom for believing in me.

Chapter One

Present Day - London, England

With a quick peek around to make sure no one was paying any mind, Lucy Merriweather bent down to tie her shoe and kissed the ground. "Hello, England. I've waited a very long time to meet you," she whispered.

"Come along, Lucy, the car is waiting." Lord Blackford, otherwise known as Simon Grey, peered over his shoulder in exasperation.

One last peek at the private jet they'd boarded in North Carolina then Lucy looked to the heavens. *Please let this trip take away my doubts.* Really. It was too nice of a day to worry. Worries could always wait for another day. A smile tugged at her face as she practically skipped over to Simon.

"Where are they?" Lucy rummaged around in the large messenger bag for a pair of blissfully dark sunglasses. A moment later she slid them up on her head as she settled into the plush, darkened interior of the waiting sedan.

Things were moving too fast. It seemed like only yesterday a friend of her sister set Lucy up on a blind date. Surprisingly enough, the date led to a relationship and then a whirlwind three-month courtship, during which she often wondered why he'd chosen her. Simon was titled and rich and she was so very ordinary. They'd gotten along well enough. Then two weeks ago, after an argument about her not standing up for herself at work, he'd apologized, taken her to Duke Gardens and shocked the heck out of her with this fantastic trip. Maybe she'd been wrong about the state of their relationship.

Could he be her very own knight in shining armor? She knew there was no such thing, but it was nice to dream. Throughout her five years at college, she'd learned that lesson over and over. Various dating trials and tribulations convinced her it would be sheer luck to find someone she cared for, but she had been doubtful she'd find someone who accepted the real Lucy.

Then she met him. On the minus side of the running column in her head, Simon could be a bit distant and occasionally rude to those in the service industry. She'd decided to chalk up his behavior to her Southern upbringing versus his stiff-upper-lip English life.

In the plus column, he was financially stable, treated her okay, and she liked him more than anyone else she'd met thus far in her life. And not that it should be a factor, but come on, he *lived in England.* Had the charming accent going for him.

Simon was a real, living, breathing lord, and that was so much better than an imaginary knight. Given her luck, any knight she did encounter would not only be smelly but ride an even smellier horse and probably wear tarnished armor she'd end up polishing. All while worrying the roof over their heads would collapse on them while they slept. *Dramatic much?*

So what if Simon didn't make her heart go pitter-patter like the heroines in the books she secretly read on her e-reader? True love was a fairy tale. Airbrushed and marketed to make you think it was perfect so you would spend your life searching, only to find out it was a big fat scam. Kinda like seeing models and celebrities without makeup or Photoshop. What a letdown.

Security trumped make-believe and passion every day of the week. Lucy sighed. She was already making excuses for him, and the whole purpose of this trip was to decide if she'd accept him, niggling worries and all, or end things and move on with her life.

Twice she'd tried to end the relationship and both times he'd talked her out of it. Apologized for whatever it was that upset her and bought her flowers. The man could charm the trunk off an elephant when he put his mind to it. His single-mindedness, normally a trait she was in awe of, now filled her with nervousness. She'd seen the faded red leather box in his carry-on.

Curiosity made her look. The glittering ring had to be the family heirloom he'd mentioned in conversation a few weeks back. The thing was enormous and gave her a panic attack just looking at it. Or maybe the panic attack came when she imagined if they stayed together…the weight of all those centuries of history pressing down on her until there was nothing left.

A prickling sensation ran down the back of her ear, and she smothered a giggle at the ridiculous thought. What did she have to worry about? The ring wasn't a factor yet. After all, she wasn't even sure she wanted to stay with a man who didn't give up his seat for a pregnant woman or grandmother. And she'd witnessed both. But then again, everyone had their quirks and flaws. This vacation was to help her decide what she really wanted in a partner.

And so yesterday she'd boarded Simon's jet, and now here she was. In England. A place she'd dreamed about for as long as she could remember. Longed to visit but never could afford. Too much late night British television convinced her England was where she belonged. Lucy pinched the skin in the crook of her arm and suppressed a yelp. Nope, not dreaming.

"All right, darling?"

Heat suffused her chest and face. "Fine. Must've banged my elbow on the door."

He patted her knee and went back to typing out emails on his mobile, leaving her free to soak up the scenery.

Not wanting to look like a complete tourist with nose pressed to the glass, drooling on the sumptuous cream-colored leather upholstery, Lucy slid her sunglasses down to hide how wide-eyed she must look. So far England was everything she'd imagined and more. A glow of happiness radiated through her like the golden summer sun on Holden Beach back home as they drove through the streets of London.

The ride to Simon's home went by way too fast. The driver carried the luggage inside the old stone building. The juxtaposition of old exterior meets modern interior was jarring. The flat was as modern and uncluttered as the man. Eyeing the plush white carpet with a frown, she slipped off her shoes, sank in up to her ankles and proceeded to examine the expansive room. White walls, chrome and glass tables. And, gulp, white furniture too. Guess there wouldn't be any popcorn and red wine while she enjoyed her favorite television shows, unless she covered the pristine furniture with towels.

The only signs of color came from the large abstract paintings and metal sculptures placed here and there, and huge windows overlooking the lovely boutiques and restaurants in Knightsbridge. How on earth did he keep the place clean? She'd been brought up with a housekeeper. Most Southern women had a cleaning service or housekeeper, but his cleaning lady must be amazing. Or maybe he was so neat he never made a mess. *Better not ever let him see your craft room.* Even the few magazines on the ugly coffee table were lined up with military precision. They didn't look like they'd ever been read.

"No pets?"

"All that dreadful hair?" Simon shuddered. "I'm allergic. Had a fish once as a boy."

The sinking feeling in her stomach made Lucy stumble. No pets? She was planning on getting another cat after her beloved Doodlebug had passed away several months ago. Could she be with someone who didn't like animals? Another item in the maybe column.

With another dubious look at the white furniture, she hoped the sainted cleaning lady came every day. While Lucy didn't like to leave dirty dishes in the sink, she certainly didn't mind a bit of clutter to make the place look lived in. His space looked like the cover of a magazine. A light hand on her arm made her flinch, and she brushed away the worry.

"It's very white and modern," she ventured.

"I'm pleased you approve, darling. Shall we make our way to the shops after you've settled in?"

"Yes. And tea. I've always wanted afternoon tea at Harrods."

"Certainly. There's a new place I thought perhaps we'd try for dinner. Then tomorrow after luncheon we depart for Blackford Castle, so no lazing about in the morning."

Mentally congratulating herself for finally saving enough money for such a trip, Lucy happily pondered doing some serious damage at the shops. Simon insisted on paying for the trip, and she finally quit offering after he'd scowled at her, and simply decided to enjoy the trip. And really study the man in her life in his own habitat, so to speak.

Hastily touching up her makeup in the luxurious, all-white marble bath, she stuck her tongue out at the reflection in the mirror.

Cosmetics and brushes lay scattered across the counter as she dashed out to the living room, a pair of pretty but comfortable sandals dangling from two fingers.

The shopping was everything she'd hoped for, the tea divine and dinner so delicious she swore she'd gained a pound. Simon was polite and charming and didn't say a word when she ate all her dessert and half of his. Sprawled across a large chair, she reached down and unbuttoned the button on her pants. Much better.

Introverted and quiet, she'd found dating nonexistent during high school and disastrous during college. Upon graduation, she'd landed a job writing product documentation for a company located clear across the country. The company was small and it didn't pay much, but she got to telecommute and set her own hours. Not dealing with traffic or a tiny, drab cubicle was worth making less money. Left to her own devices over the next year, Lucy found it easier and easier to withdraw from an agonizing social scene. Both of her sisters tried to get her to come out with them, to meet people, do things. But after the millionth time of begging her to join them, they finally got the message and stopped asking.

A sharp pang hit her in the side, and she pressed her fist into the soft flesh to stop the pain. This was the first time Lucy had been outside of the United States. She missed her sisters, Charlotte and Melinda, and her Aunt Pittypat. Worried over losing them too. They were the only family she had left.

Bright sunlight penetrated her eyelids. A muffled voice drew her attention. "...running out of time...it has to be Friday." The sound faded and she blinked several times, yawning without covering her mouth. A quiet giggle left her lips before she looked toward the bedroom to see if he'd seen her. Nope. The crick in her neck and shoulders told her she'd fallen asleep in the chair last night. With a groan and several unladylike creaks, Lucy stood and stretched, her crochet hook and ball of yarn falling to the floor.

"Good morning, darling. I didn't want to wake you last night. You looked so peaceful where you were sleeping." Simon kissed her cheek and handed her a cup of tea.

The warmth slid down her throat, waking her fully as she looked him over. He was on the short side for a man, at five foot six. They were the same height. Luckily, he didn't seem to care if she wore heels, making her taller than him. He had light brown eyes, honey-blond hair cut short and a lean runner's body.

Simon was nothing like Carl, the boyfriend of her oldest sister, Melinda. Carl was a Grade-A jerk who hit on anything female, including Lucy and her youngest sister Charlotte.

No, Simon never looked at other women.

Add one to the plus column. When he turned on the charm, like yesterday when he ran into Lady Something or other he'd known as a child…my oh my, the man could beguile an alligator into becoming a vegetarian.

Tea finished, she stood, mouth open, gazing at the shower. Somehow she hadn't noticed it yesterday when they'd arrived. Three showerheads ensured she'd spend too much time luxuriating under the hot, soothing spray while Simon made more calls. He was part owner of a polo team. Maybe she'd get to take in a polo match while they were here. She wondered, was a fancy hat required to attend?

Dressed and feeling like the fog had finally lifted from her brain, Lucy enjoyed the breakfast delivered that morning. Fruit and tea and a bagel. Still warm and smothered in cream cheese. Heaven. As she was starting on the second half, Simon cleared his throat.

"No more bagels for a while." He patted his flat stomach and looked her over. "Can't let ourselves go to pot. I've noticed you've put on a bit of weight recently."

Hot all over, Lucy glanced down at the rest of the bagel on her plate, and with a longing glance pushed it to the side. She knew she wasn't skinny. Maybe she could stand to lose ten pounds, but she wasn't overweight. Average. Yep, totally average in body and looks. So why worry while they were on vacation? Not going to happen. This was her vacation and she planned to enjoy herself…when he wasn't watching. Once she was back home, she'd buckle down and watch what she ate. She shot a guilty look toward the pot of hot chocolate on the counter and sat on her hands. When he was busy with work later then she'd enjoy a small cup. Men. The man probably forbade a single extra pound to adhere to his body.

Relationships were about compromise. If they stayed together she'd have to step it up a notch. To be perfectly honest, she'd have to start exercising. Her idea of exercise was going for a leisurely walk, but Simon loved to play polo and tennis, run *and* go sailing. The thought of all that effort made her sneak a cup of the decadent hot chocolate and sip it while she finished getting ready.

Simon took her on a brief tour around London before they headed out of the city in another big black sedan. The buildings gave way to adorable fairy-tale towns, and then to the greenest earth she'd ever laid eyes on. The idyllic countryside flew by, and she stayed turned in her seat to stare out the window. But she did not drool on the glass. Okay, maybe a little. Fluffy sheep grazed in pastures, horses pranced about, and the charming cottages with wildflowers growing everywhere made her lust over each and every one they passed.

Oblivious, Simon spoke in low tones on his ever-present mobile. Lucy owned a phone but didn't plan on turning it on until absolutely necessary. She'd called to let her sisters know she arrived safely and promised to call when she returned home. Content to enjoy the day, she soaked in every detail as they sped toward their destination.

Simon ended the call and kissed her on the cheek. "Sorry, darling. Dreadfully boring work details."

"Are we close to York? Is that where we're going?"

"Blackford is situated on the coast overlooking the North Sea. It's about…let's see, in miles, forty miles from York."

Lucy turned and snuggled into his shoulder. "The countryside is beautiful. Would you tell me about your family home? I don't think we've ever talked about it."

"My ancestor took Blackford Castle by force from a traitor to the crown in 1307. The Grey family has held it ever since. It's not a large castle. The majority of the buildings have fallen into ruin. Ghastly expensive to keep up the place." He shifted, crossing his legs.

"You own a castle?" Lucy gaped at him. Talk about one for the plus side of her boyfriend column.

He reached up, placing a finger under her chin, and pushed her mouth shut. "Blackford was a Norman stronghold. Built in 1178. Each owner added on to the place until the castle was completed in 1313. It isn't much to look at now, but back in its prime it was a forbidding place. A fortress. I hope you shall enjoy the old pile of stone." Simon gave a small half-shrug, shifted in his seat again and patted her hand.

"It sounds delightful."

"Useless is more like it." He glanced at his mobile and went on. "Blackford was abandoned in 1317, and as time passed it was presumed to be haunted. Rather absurd in this day and age, wouldn't you agree?"

Before she could answer, he'd rolled down the window and

shouted, "Come on, move along." He leaned back in the window. "Fred, sound the horn. Get them going."

Sheep surrounded the sedan, ignoring the beeps from the horn. A young boy waved at them and tried to move the beasts along.

"I'm sure they'll be out of the way soon enough. It's not like we're in a hurry."

"Stupid kid," he muttered.

The wind made a keening sound and Lucy gulped, imagining a green lady appearing as she rounded a corner of the castle. She tugged his arm so he'd quit scowling out the window.

"Is Blackford really haunted?"

"Don't be ridiculous. Of course not. An ancestor came up with the idea to keep people away, and it's worked wonderfully well. With the place falling down, it isn't safe, and I'd hate for someone to get hurt exploring."

Relieved, she tucked a strand of hair behind her ear.

"You own a castle, a piece of history. Don't you have any desire to rebuild? Live in the home of your ancestors?"

He looked horrified at the idea. "In that drafty old pile of stones? There's only one wing intact. The expense would bankrupt me." Simon made a face.

"All those unclean people living inside the walls for hundreds of years." He shuddered. "Not to mention the astronomical cost of heating the place and hiring staff. I'd be broke in a year. There's a cottage on the grounds where we'll stay overnight. I wanted you to know my family, even if it's only through our history."

She reached up to touch his face. "I'm sorry you're the only one left. I wish my parents were still here. I miss them every day." She sneezed three times. "I'm sure your parents were very proud of you."

Simon handed her a soft handkerchief from the pocket of immaculate navy slacks. "What would I do without you, Lucy?"

She sniffed. "I'm glad I said yes to the blind date."

"It was fate." He smoothed her hair back and pulled her close.

The drive through the village was charming. The few shops, pub and other assorted businesses clustered together inside the village along the main road. Old cottages dotted the countryside, making her feel as if she'd stepped back in time. What would it be like to live here?

Simon pointed ahead of them, and when she turned to look, a shiver ran down her spine, as if one of her sisters had dropped a handful of ice down the back of her shirt. Sadness seemed to permeate the very air as they approached Simon's ancestral home.

"Blackford Castle. Not the largest holding, but the grounds are extensive."

"You were right, it's very forbidding."

The car came to a stop in front of a tiny cottage. The smell of the sea made her inhale deeply. One of her favorite smells in all the world. Simon was looking at the cottage with a frown as they stepped out of the car.

"It's small but serviceable. I sent instructions to air the place out. A group of women from the village come weekly to clean, and there's a caretaker who lives on the western edge of the grounds. If you need anything while we're here, let Carson know."

Lucy couldn't tear her eyes away from the hauntingly beautiful ruins. She wanted to cry looking up at the place. It seemed lonely and filled with sadness. For a moment she felt dizzy, a sense of déjà vu passing over her. Which was ridiculous, as she'd never been out of the States. She shook herself, tore her gaze away from the battlements and pointed to the tiny cottage.

"It's straight out of a fairy tale." And it was, with its thatched roof and overgrown garden. She could live here and be happy. Bet there wasn't a single piece of white furniture or carpet in the whole place.

"At one time I thought of turning it into a gift shop and charging admission to the ruins, but after running the numbers I decided against it."

As Simon opened the door to the cottage, a big black bird flew out. He threw his hands up, dancing around and emitting what Lucy would have called a shriek. But that wouldn't be very nice to say. A laugh escaped and she clapped a hand over her mouth to hold in another. Red-faced, Simon brushed himself off, hair mussed and panting.

"Did you see? Damned raven almost took my head off. I despise ravens. Filthy birds."

Lucy bit the inside of her cheek, hard. "You probably scared him." If she laughed, he'd think she was making fun of him and pout the rest of the day.

"Right." He smoothed his hair down and shot her a suspicious look. Guess she better work on her poker face.

"Fred, bring the bags inside."

The silent driver nodded and Lucy let Simon lead the way. The door opened the rest of the way with a loud groan. Simon wrinkled his nose.

"It's outdated and fussy, but it'll do for the one night."

"It's absolutely charming. I love it."

The driver stood stiffly outside the doorway.

"Anything else, my lord?"

"That will be all. I'll…we'll be going back to London tomorrow. Be here at ten."

With a nod, the driver motored down the lane and they were alone. Lucy couldn't wait to explore the small cottage with its chintz furniture and linen curtains fluttering in the warm summer breeze.

Fluttering? Lucy blinked and the curtains were still. A small laugh escaped as she realized old houses were drafty. There wasn't any such thing as a ghost. With a small twirl, she turned to pull

Simon along but stopped, her hand held out in midair.

Simon looked nervous. He was never nervous. She was about to ask him what was wrong, but he took her by the arm, not noticing her hand already hanging in the air like a bent tree limb, and dragged her over to one of the chairs. A puff of dust exploded when she sat, and she sneezed three times. He grimaced and brushed dust off his slacks before kneeling beside her.

"Darling, I know it's only been a few months, but you are the only one for me. Make me the happiest man in England and marry me."

Chapter Two

"I don't know what to say." Lucy eyed the sparkling ring.

Simon knelt beside her and fidgeted with his cufflink.

"Say yes. And then tomorrow night we'll be married in the great hall of Blackford Castle."

She sat there staring dumbly down at him as every moment of their time together flashed before her eyes. Lucy clapped a hand over her mouth, jumped up from the chair and ran outside. Over and over she heaved into the lovely rosebushes by the front door. Skin clammy, she wiped her forehead with her shirt and leaned against the cool stone wall of the cottage.

"Darling, are you ill?"

Simon started to pull her close, caught a whiff of the stench and made a face of disgust. "Must have been all the lunch you consumed. You ate way too much. It has made you ill."

He took her by the hand, leading her around the cottage to a chair. Grateful, she leaned back, taking shallow breaths though her mouth.

"I'll get you some water."

He returned with a bottle of water, and for a second, she thought maybe she'd change her mind.

"Thank you." The reality of him asking made everything clear. She'd overlooked his condescending attitude and mean remarks to her because of the way he could be so solicitous and charming. The way it sounded when he called her *darling* in his sexy English accent. But they weren't compatible. Didn't have the same values or want the same things out of life. He was money and modern and obsessed with fitness. She believed you worked to live, ate dessert first and loved everything old. This man was not the one for her.

"Simon, I don't think…"

"All the arrangements have been made. I purchased the dress I saw you mooning over."

Lucy took a gulp of water. "I can't marry you."

For an instant she swore he looked furious, but then he smiled and she could see the charm oozing out of him. "Don't be—"

Lucy held up a hand. "Please. Let me finish."

She took a deep breath, her stomach settling down now that she'd accepted her decision.

"You'll make someone a wonderful husband. But not me. We're too different. You're modern and love to exercise and hate animals and small children. Not to mention, we have different ideas of how people should be treated. You wouldn't be happy with me."

He turned his most dazzling smile on her and stood to pace. "I know we're different. Don't you see? You keep me grounded. And yes, I believe those of a lower social rank deserve different treatment than those of my own social class. You'll get used to me."

He looked at Blackford. "You can keep a pet here at the cottage. Perhaps a horse. Would that make you happy? Think what a delightful story to tell our sons about how I proposed here at the family estate. For I must have an heir and a spare."

She could see why the man in front of her was so successful. He simply ignored what he didn't want to hear and moved forward.

"It's tradition, you know."

At a loss, she tilted her head to look at him. "What is?"

"Each member of the Grey family brings his or her intended to the castle to marry. Only the two of them. And the priest, of course. Then they spend the night in the only room still intact and celebrate with a private brunch the following day." He held out his hands, looking earnest and worried. "Afterwards, we'll invite your sisters to London for a smashing party."

"But—"

"The family tradition goes back hundreds of years…I know it's rather laughable in this day and age, but there's a prophecy." He looked out the window toward the castle currently under discussion.

"The prophecy decrees in order to have a long-lasting, happy marriage with an heir—"

She noted he stumbled over the words *long-lasting*.

"—we must marry under the roof of Blackford Castle and spend our wedding night within the walls. It will be like camping. You Americans enjoy camping."

She waved away the comment. And no, she most certainly did not like to camp. Her idea of camping was a hotel without room service. A castle without running water or electricity? Forget it.

"You're not listening to me. I should have ended things sooner, but I thought maybe seeing you in your own country, feeling at home, I'd see the real you. And I realized this *is* the real you. I wish things were different. I'm sorry, Simon. I can't marry you."

He gathered her into his arms and patted her hair. After a few minutes passed, Simon stepped back and gazed into her eyes, the saddest expression she'd ever seen gracing his face.

His voice was barely a whisper. "I'm terribly sorry you feel that way, darling. We would make a good marriage together. Why don't you take the day to think about it and we can discuss our plans over dinner?"

He slid the ring over her knuckle, and Lucy felt the weight of countless years tightening around her finger. The ring shifted, and for a moment she thought it would fly off her finger and roll away as if it didn't want to be there. She snorted. *Well, I don't want to wear you either, but we'll humor him until dinner.*

For the first time, in a long time, she'd stood up for herself. It felt good.

The rest of the day passed quickly. Lucy made it to the village before yanking the heavy ring off her finger and shoving it in a pocket. Shoulders squared back, she told herself for the umpteenth time, *He's not the one for you.*

The small village was delightful. The fish and chips from a street vendor divine, and she was content to wander in and out of shops and up and down the old streets, happy to soak up a new experience.

It would have been perfect to live here, to make the small cottage her own. Getting married to a man you didn't love? The cost was too high. Truth be told, she wanted someone who loved her for her. A man who used his actions, not a bunch of pretty words. Lucy rubbed her temples, feeling old at twenty-four. There had to be a man out there for her. Wasn't there someone for everyone? Did her one and only live in some remote country she'd never visit?

Back at the cottage, she opened the door, wincing when it hit the wall with a bang.

"Did you enjoy your time in the village, darling?"

She was unsurprised to see an elaborate dinner laid out on the scarred wooden table.

"It was picture-postcard perfect." A chair beckoned, and she sank into it. "You didn't have to go to all this trouble."

"We must eat. I thought a nice dinner and conversation would be a perfect way to end the day." Simon smiled the smile of a predator just before it pounced. "I've even turned my mobile off. I know how much you hate it when I take calls during dinner."

She blinked, wondering if she'd heard him correctly. He never turned his phone off. Once she heard him in the bathroom doing his business. Poop, by the loud noises. He was holding a conversation. The man would be first in line when some company invented cellular implants. Simon stood in front of her wearing his sweetest smile. The one that usually made her give in to whatever they disagreed on. *Be strong. You've made your decision. Don't let him charm you into changing your mind all because you want to live in a cottage by a ruined castle. In England.*

"Would you care for a glass of champagne?" He gestured to a large silver bucket on the sideboard.

"I'd love one, thanks."

He smiled and popped the cork. The faint smell of bubbles filled the air. "You look so beautiful, darling. Your eyes are the color of fine silver. They were the first thing I noticed about you."

The chair creaked as Lucy squirmed. Something sharp poked her in the hip. The ring. She leaned back so she could wriggle her fingers in the pocket of her jeans. The ring sparkled in the palm of her hand. As she laid it on the table with a click, she heard a raven calling outside the window.

"If you want me to leave now, I will. Please know I've given your proposal a great deal of thought. I'm certain of my decision." She took a deep, fortifying breath.

"Please don't try and change my mind. I'm sorry I agreed to the trip when I had concerns about us…I thought it would be a good way to see if we were truly suited. You need someone who wants the same things in life as you. I'm not her."

He took the ring, pocketed it then placed a kiss on the top of her head.

"While I shall never recover from the rejection, I have decided I will not be angry. Perhaps it is best to know now instead of having children and putting them through a dreadful divorce years later."

This was a change. Her forehead crinkled as she waited for him to say he wanted her to leave. Simon remained quiet. Maybe they could have a nice dinner, and when they returned to London tomorrow she'd book a ticket back home.

He refilled the glasses. "Let's enjoy dinner, drink our champagne and forget I even asked."

She relaxed a little and took a sip of champagne, stopping to enjoy how the bubbles tickled her nose.

"Tomorrow I'll ready the jet to take you home. No hard feelings." Simon handed her a chocolate-covered strawberry.

Relief swept through her. So he wasn't the right guy, but at least he was taking her rejection like the well-mannered lord she'd thought he was when they first met.

She would act like a grownup as well. "I appreciate it."

With the worry banished, Lucy relaxed and enjoyed the sumptuous meal. The conversation flowed, and Simon was his most charming self. Every time she blinked he was refilling the glass. Bleary-eyed, Lucy giggled.

"I better stop drinking. I'm tipsy." She stood, and for a moment wobbled as the room tilted before she gained her balance. Teetering over to the window overlooking Blackford Castle, Lucy tripped, sloshing champagne onto the floor.

"Oops."

"We're both rather pissed." He raised a glass. "We won't be needing the bubbly for our nuptials, so let's pop another bottle. Bottoms up and all that rot."

Things started to go fuzzy and dark around the edges. Through a gauzy curtain she watched the glass slipping from her fingers, hitting the floor and shattering.

Someone must've stuck cotton in her ears. So not funny. Lucy shook her head and blinked. Simon stood before her holding a large box in his arms. What on earth?

"I know we're not suited to each other." He opened the first box, pulling out the most beautiful pair of crystal-encrusted blue wedge heels she'd ever seen.

"I bought these hoping you would say yes. I'd like you to have them anyway." With a flourish, the lid came off a much larger box, revealing a stunning dress. A sparkly fit for a princess dress that looked very much like a wedding gown. The same gown she'd pinned on Pinterest.

"I don't understand. We're breaking up—why would you give me my fantasy wedding dress?" The alcohol made everything seem like a dream. Had she fallen asleep and was dreaming?

"I respect your decision. Though wouldn't it be fun to wear the dress? Pretend we're getting married?"

"Fun isn't the word I'd use."

Simon took her hands in his. "Pretend we're in a play. I may never meet the right woman. At least this way I can tell myself I didn't stomp on tradition, even if it is a fake wedding." He looked into her eyes and a tear ran down his cheek.

"Please, Lucy. I know I'm drunk, but please, won't you do this one silly thing for me?"

Maybe it was the champagne or his tear. In the three months they'd been dating, she'd never seen Simon upset, let alone cry. Seeing his tears made her feel like a jerk for smashing all of his carefully laid-out plans to bits. She hiccupped. Why not play along? It was make-believe.

"Oh, all right, I'll do it."

With a whoop of laughter, Simon spun her around.

"Wait, put me down before I barf."

Simon beamed at her gently, setting her back on solid ground. "I'll change and be waiting in the great hall. This will be so much fun, darling."

He made a call on his mobile, and a minute later two of the cleaning women appeared in the doorway, waving to Simon as he left.

Before Lucy could protest, she was dressed in the stunning gown and hurried into the waiting car for the short drive up to the castle. They were getting fake-married on Thursday. June twenty-first. The first day of summer. A day she would have picked for her real wedding.

Hadn't she read some old rhyme? Something about *Wednesday the best day of all. Thursday for losses?* Was it a bad omen? She snorted. It was silly to believe in things like ghosts and omens. Or, for that matter, that it was good luck to have rain on your wedding day. Even if it was a fake wedding. It kinda felt real.

Simon would be waiting in the great hall. It was dark, so the castle didn't come into view until they were right in front of it. She wrinkled her nose. The place looked menacing and creepy. As if something bad was biding its time deep within the stone, ready to eat her should she set foot in the place. Her laugh filled the car, startling the driver.

"Everything all right?"

"Too much to drink, making me think silly thoughts. I'm fine." She mentally smacked herself. *Get it together—you're letting your emotions and horribly overactive imagination get the best of you. You're doing this to make Simon feel better. It's fake but obviously important to him, so pull it together. There's nothing scary here. It's a pile of stone.*

Lucy stared up at the battlements, tracing them against the rain-spattered window with her index finger. More like abandoned and unloved rather than malevolent.

The driver held a huge umbrella to shield her from the raindrops. She made it out of the car and into the gatehouse without getting a drop on the perfect dress.

Lucy pointed up at the portcullis. "Does that still work?"

The driver grinned. "Both of them do. Though don't worry—there aren't any archers waiting to shoot you dead." He rapped on the stone. "Walls are ten feet thick and go four feet into the ground, so they couldn't be tunneled under."

So maybe she shouldn't have asked. His words went in her head, swirled around then flew out her ear into the night. "Castle buff, are you?" She hiccupped again.

Her escort helped her over what remained of a wall. "One of my ancestors worked in the stables." He kept a hand on her arm to keep her steady.

She was smashed. He helped her through the gatehouse, across the courtyard and up the steps of the keep. Chunks of stone tumbled about, and Lucy resisted the urge to pat the gaping wall. If the castle were hers, she'd restore it. Live in it and be happy. Too bad she'd told him she wouldn't marry him.

Shrugging out of the Hunter rain boots and into the beautiful pair of four-inch wedge heels, she gave thanks that the keep still had a partial roof to shield the icy white dress. It was sleeveless and hugged her curves, and was covered in tiny crystals and chiffon, making her feel every inch the lady of the castle.

While Lucy might not believe in fairy tales, every girl wanted to look like a princess on her wedding day. Even if it was only a fake wedding. Was it bad luck to have a fake wedding?

The thought rattled around in her fuzzy brain before she decided participating in a make-believe wedding to make her now ex-boyfriend happy was no different than acting in a play.

The driver handed her flowers.

"Thanks. Seems a bit much for a charade."

The bouquet was simple, made up of colorful wildflowers from the surrounding area. The women had twisted her long brown hair up into a French twist and added sparkly crystal flower pins to coordinate with her jewelry.

Rose petals? Bit much. Guess he had everything planned and figured he might as well use it. The smell of the roses filled her nose as she walked through the cavernous room. Simon stood waiting dressed in a tux, looking totally hot. She stumbled over a loose stone. The champagne had gone to her head. Time seemed to be accelerating.

"A vision of loveliness. I am truly the luckiest man in all of England to be marrying you."

Time to get into character. She smiled at her fake husband-to-be and took a deep breath. In the morning they'd laugh about all this on the way back to London.

"Wait." A cold blast of air made her shiver. "He looks like a real priest."

Simon shook his head at the man. "He's an actor."

"You're really taking this to extremes."

"Please, darling."

The vows were said in record time. The little priest kept nervously glancing around the hall as if worried the devil himself would appear out of the stone to snatch him down to the fiery underworld.

The priest solemnly intoned, "May your joys be as bright as your beloved homeland sun, your years of happiness as numerous as the grains of sand on the beach and your troubles vanish in the sunlight of your love. You may kiss the bride."

Those were the same lines she'd saved on her computer. He must have been looking through her files.

Simon pulled her close, giddy excitement on his face, and laid the sloppiest kiss ever on her. In a daze, her mind tried to warn her something was off. Simon was never giddy. Especially over a fake wedding. Lucy ignored the voice, chalking it up to nerves and too much to drink, and took his arm.

The priest puffed himself up and said to the castle, empty except for the caretaker and driver, some long, drawn-out words about the two of them. She'd heard her name and Simon's in there, but the rest seemed to swirl around her brain in a pastel-colored fog.

A crack of thunder reverberated through the room, shaking the very foundations of the castle as a stone tumbled to the cracked floor. She laughed hysterically. Did that mean the castle was ticked they'd dared to mock the sanctity of a wedding?

The priest had a quiet word with her "husband" before making the sign of the cross and scurrying off as fast as his chubby legs could carry him. Lucy swore she smelled alcohol on his breath.

"My lady, if you'll follow me?"

"How long are we staying in character?"

"Just a bit longer, darling wife."

Fine, she'd play along. "My Lord Blackford, I'd be delighted."

Simon led her up a mostly intact staircase. If she turned left she'd fall down into nothingness. Instead they turned right down a dark corridor lit by actual torches. He saw the look on her face, mouth gaping open.

"The caretaker took care of the torches, though I was in charge of our accommodations for the night." With a flourish, he opened the door. "I know there isn't much left of the place, but I think you'll approve."

Lucy blinked. "It's beautiful. Are the other rooms on this level intact? I mean, we're not together anymore. I'm not sleeping with you tonight, fake wedding or not."

"Of course not. Fred has gone back to the village for the night and it's pouring down rain. I'd hate to ruin my tux and your dress by walking back to the cottage." Simon patted her arm. "This is the only room, unless you want to sleep on the cold stone floor of the great hall."

Why had she drunk so much? She needed a clear head to understand what she was missing.

"In fact, if we'd have kept walking in the dark, we'd have found ourselves dashed to death on the rocks below and drowned in the sea. There really isn't much habitable space left. I promise no funny business. We'll each stay on our own side of the bed. In the morning you can look out the window at the breathtaking view. Lucy?"

Looked like she would be sleeping in the same bed with him. It would be awkward. Thank goodness she was drunk. "Yes?"

"Stay away from the water. There've been several drownings over the years."

She shuddered and turned her attention to the room. Candles glowed casting shadows on the wall. The bed was a huge four-poster, very masculine looking. It was covered in white bedding and pillows. What was it with him and the color white? It might be warm enough during the day, in the low to mid-sixties, but the temperature went down into the low fifties at night, and the stone walls made everything feel damp and cold. Lucy kept blinking to clear her vision. The storm raging outside wasn't helping her pounding headache. Simon had insisted on another drink to toast their nuptials. The glass slipped from her grasp and shattered on the stone floor. The sound of laughter seemed to fill the room.

Chapter Three

Flashes of images skittered across Lucy's eyelids. The back of Simon's legs. His shoulder blade banging against her cheek. Wind blowing through her dress. Cold rain stabbing her skin.

The jarring motion stopped and Lucy found herself sitting on a hard stone bench.

"Wha...where are we?" She dimly noted the beautiful dress was ruined. "Why are we outside? I thought we didn't want to get wet."

Simon wore a black raincoat as he knelt down in front of her.

"We're out on the battlements, darling. I'm dreadfully sorry, but the prophecy must be fulfilled."

The ringing in her head made it hard to concentrate. Cold stone scraped against her palm as she tried to stand before falling back and banging her shoulder against the wall. The sharp pain brought clarity.

"Why on earth are you talking about a prophecy? Tonight was a joke."

His face twisted into someone she'd never seen before. Ice encased her body, making it hard to breathe. He looked like someone she'd be afraid to run into on a dark night. She blinked at him. Had she ever known this man?

"About that. Once you had the audacity to refuse me, I had to take drastic measures." He stared into her eyes.

"I did what was necessary, drugged you. The wedding was real, although there is no romantic family tradition. I told you that rubbish knowing you'd get all cow-eyed and go along with the ruse. Pretending to marry me. You see, Lucy, I detest this pile of stone. It's an enormous drain on my trust fund, and I do so enjoy my money."

"So sell it. Who cares?" Her voice carried over the storm. "You drugged me and married me without my consent. This wedding will never stand. I'm leaving right now, finding the nearest cop and having you arrested." Her legs wouldn't hold her. She fell back against the stone, looking up at him in horror.

"The effects will wear off soon enough."

Her knee buckled as she tried to stand again. Simon laughed and her stomach heaved. "Why?"

"I cannot sell Blackford. Trust me, my ancestors and I have tried every conceivable idea, no matter how unsavory. The contract written so long ago is unbreakable. The only way to get rid of the place is to kill you."

She shook her head. "You have lost your mind. That doesn't make an ounce of sense."

The rising hysteria threatened to choke her. Lucy tried once more to stand, to take a step. It was like moving through wet concrete. *Keep him talking and escape, you idiot.*

"I'm perfectly sober. I poured my drinks out. I couldn't very well drink drugged champagne." He cocked his head at her. "You're not going anywhere until I've set things right."

"You're insane. Help! Somebody help me!"

"Scream as long and loud as you wish, darling. No one will hear you." Simon grasped her by the shoulders and pushed her into the corner of the short wall.

"You see, the prophecy states when the last of the Grey line betrays the last of the Brandon line by foul deeds for the second time, the curse shall be lifted and the castle owned no more by the Grey family."

He twitched as lightning lit up the night sky. "So in killing you, I'll be free of this place and able to enjoy my money."

Somehow Lucy didn't think a curse would work so literally. "Did you get kicked in the head by one of your polo ponies? I have two sisters. Our last name is Merriweather, not Brandon, you deranged lunatic."

She had to make her legs move and get away from him. When the next bolt of lighting lit up the sky, she looked down. Too far to jump, and the rocks looked like they'd smash her head open. Like a watermelon dropped from the back of a pickup truck onto the highway. She had to buy time until the effects of the drug wore off and she could escape.

"Your sisters. One of them will have an accident on the way to work tomorrow, and the other, well, I've always wondered what it would be like to die by fire. There's nothing you can do to save them. Your current name is Merriweather, but it wasn't always. I did my research most carefully. You, not your sisters, are descended from the Brandon line. There are no others left. I am sorry you have to die. So distasteful. Think, Lucy. Do you really think I would marry a common little boring mouse with low self-esteem such as yourself?"

Simon lunged at her with a knife. Cold air and rain blew across her ribcage. Frantically she patted her tummy. He'd sliced the dress and just barely nicked her. A tiny drop of blood welled up. She gathered every ounce of strength, willing her foot to work. The kick was pitiful, though he jumped back, baring his teeth at her. Before she could try again, he stomped on her ankle. Pain exploded through her body and she heaved.

He wrinkled his nose. "Disgusting. And that dreadful accent. My God, if I never hear another Southern accent again, it will be too soon."

Simon sniffed down his nose at her, and in a blinding flash all of the little niggling worries came crashing down. How he looked down on others, the disgusted look on his face when he thought she wasn't looking and stories he'd told of bettering his classmates.

She'd been blinded. By his charm, accent and the fact that someone seemingly normal wanted her. Confused snobbery with politeness. What a fool. Why hadn't she trusted her gut? Now she'd been tricked into marrying him, all so he could kill her. Obviously, she was having a nightmare brought on by too much to drink.

Quick as a snake, he pulled her to her feet and pushed. Lucy's arms windmilled, grasping at air as the heavy dress kept her from going over.

"Simon, no!"

Thunder cracked, the rain poured down and when lighting next lit up the sky, absurdly, she was upset that the dream dress was utterly ruined. Was she going into shock? In the movies, characters experienced random thoughts. Must be what was happening to her. Lighting flashed. Time seemed to stretch out and stop. She saw a dark indent on the top of the stone wall and lunged for anything to hold on to.

"Goodbye, Lucy." Simon grabbed her legs to heave her over the wall and one sparkly blue shoe went skittering across the stone. In moments, she'd be smashed to bits or drowned, unless she did something. The night turned to day with the next flash, and she reached again for the dark spot that, strangely enough, looked like a bloodstain instead of a handhold. Was it her blood? Had he already killed her?

As her fingers skimmed across the dark mark searching for something to grab on to, lightning flashed so close she saw the imprint every time she blinked. A sound like metal being torn in two made her teeth ache. A rainbow of light exploded behind her eyelids and then she was falling. After that there was no sound at all.

I need air. Can't breathe.

Lucy struggled to see through the pelting rain. Simon's face hovered inches from hers, transformed into that of a monster. The ugliness inside had seeped out, making him ugly on the outside. His smile morphed into a sneer, the skin stretched taut so the bones seemed to show through.

Nothing she did had any effect. Simon had her pinned to the cold stone, and no matter how hard she bucked, kicked and clawed at him, he wouldn't let go. His soft hands felt like a python slowly squeezing out every precious breath. Black and purple spots danced with the raindrops across her eyelids. Her heart skipped a beat and then another, slowing down.

"Die and free my family from this wretched curse."

As if through a long tunnel, she heard the muffled sound of thunder and metal scraping against stone. The next flash of lightning illuminated what looked like the blade of a sword arcing down toward her head. With her strength gone, Lucy sent up a plea: *Let it be painless.*

Metal screamed, lightning flashed and the blackness welcomed her with open arms.

Rough hands shook Lucy hard enough to rattle the fillings in her teeth. "Leave me alone," she croaked, swatting at the hand gripping her shoulder. A fit of coughing caused her to gasp in pain. Gingerly she touched her throat. It felt warm to the touch, and hurt worse than any sore throat she'd ever had.

Combined with a stuffy nose and the feeling of nails stabbing into her skull, realization sank in. Massive hangover. *That's what you get for drinking so much, lightweight.* Gruff voices filled the air. With supreme effort, she squinted to see who was so incredibly annoying so early in the morning.

Why was she wet? The beautiful dress was ruined. There were red streaks on her dress and the ground around her. It looked like blood. A squeak was all that came out when she desperately wanted to scream. Another squeak escaped her lips as the events of last night came rushing back, a movie on fast forward behind her eyes.

Was she dead? Had Simon strangled her? Or cut off her head? That would explain so much blood. Maybe she was looking down on her body right now. The big hands on her person and the male voices made her think not, but maybe it was a hallucination. Or she was in a coma in some hospital. Or the authorities had arrived, which would be excellent news. She scrubbed a hand over her face and sat the rest of the way up with a grunt.

"Ow!" The word rasped out of swollen lips. "What?" Obviously not dead or in hospital.

Her entire face hurt. Hell, her entire body felt broken and bruised. Something crusty covered her nose, cheek and part of her lip. The throbbing ache had her wincing as tears leaked down her face.

Sunrise turned the silver swords of the three men standing in front of her to a burnished rose. As she shifted to the side, her hand made contact with something rubbery.

The scream emanating from her throat sounded as if it belonged to something inhuman. A man lay next to her, eyes open and unseeing. A pool of liquid the color of ripe blackberries surrounded his head. When a fly landed in the sticky substance, the blood drained from her face. It was blood, and this man, whoever he was, was dead. How did his blood end up all over her dress? Insides heaving as a metallic taste filled her mouth, Lucy leaned over and retched. The smell of champagne and sick filled the air. Over and over she heaved until there was nothing left, her bruised throat burning as fresh tears rolled down her face.

Something sharp pricked her chest. "Ouch!" Several swords were pointing at her person, and a fleeting thought crossed her mind: wouldn't it be the perfect end to a dreadful night if she'd fallen through time? But that was simply the dramatic part of her thinking. Though talk about a night to remember.

Voices penetrated the horror in front of her. Lucy reached through the blades for the closest man's sleeve and jerked down. Hysteria bubbled up and spilled out.

"Please help me, he tried to k…k…kill me." She pointed to the blood on her dress. "I don't know what happened. I can't remember. I know I didn't hurt this man. I don't even know who he is." She gestured to the man beside her, making sure to avert her eyes from all the blood and breathe through her mouth.

"Call the police. They have to arrest Simon. He must have killed this man." Another fit of coughing racked her body.

The man snatched his arm back, and they all spoke at once. Had she banged her head? It wasn't English they were practically shouting. French, maybe? Tourists? Or some kind of re-enactors? Why hadn't she paid more attention in French class? Right, because she had a crush on Noah. Wonder what ever happened to him?

Lucy remembered how to say hello and thank you, but the rest was long gone from disuse. Falling apart gave way to anger. Her emotions were cycling faster than an instructor leading a spin class.

"Someone summon the authorities." All she remembered was Simon trying to kill her and then…the flash of something. Metal and pain. *Where was Simon?*

The men pulled her to her feet, where she stood swaying for a moment, then pointed at her chest. "Bonjour. I'm Lucy Merriweather. I need help."

She made a walking gesture on her palm by moving her pointer and index fingers. "Help. Away from here. Back to the village. Merci."

More incomprehensible words and then one of them shoved her as the others clustered around, brandishing swords, yelling and pointing to their dead friend. For the dead man was dressed the same. They all wore long blue shirts and tights.

More yelling ensued. She suddenly realized that since she was covered in the dead man's blood, they thought she'd murdered the man. Anger gave way to fear as her muddled brain tried to process the strange scene.

Lucy stomped hard on the closest man's foot with her heel. She pulled out of his grasp, yelping as her forearm started to burn, hitched up the bedraggled dress and ran. Or rather minced, the dress being so formfitting there was no way she could run. A door beckoned at the end of the battlements. She wrenched it open and ran into a solid wall before bouncing back and landing hard on her butt.

The man looming over her was scary. Dark brown hair framed a harsh face. Eyes the lush green of the English countryside glared at her, and his nose, well, it looked like it'd been broken more than once. The man said something in French and scowled down at her.

One of the men behind her called out, a stream of words she couldn't understand, and the man in front of her narrowed his eyes, demanding something from her. He grabbed her arm, fingers pressing into the soft flesh.

He looked like he was about to give an order to chop off her head. The words came out tumbling over one another. "Ouch, you're hurting me. Parlez-vous English? I'm not part of this re-enactment. We have to call the authorities. I don't know what happened to your colleague. But please, I need your phone so I can save my sisters. He said they'd be dead by morning. Don't you understand? He drugged me, tricked me into marrying him, tried to kill me and then I woke up next to some dead mystery man and I will make Simon pay. I swear it." Lucy started to hiccup.

He grunted and motioned for the grabby men with pointy swords to come forward. She scrabbled to her feet, punched the terrifying man in the stomach as hard as she could, darted under his arm and hopped into the dimly lit corridor.

"Merde."

Yep, she was right, it was French. That wasn't a very nice word, either. She might not speak the language, but everyone knew all the good swear words. Stupid re-enactors. Did they think she was the damsel in distress waiting to be rescued from the dragon? If they did, shouldn't they be rescuing her instead of trying to poke her with swords that looked and felt awfully real?

Lucy snorted. No way was she a damsel in distress. She would get herself out of this mess, thank you very much. Whatever happened after Simon tried to kill her, she was no longer mousy and introverted. Nope, she would be strong and brave...at least that was the plan.

The poor dead man must have fallen in the storm and hit his head. She'd never seen a dead person before. Okay, she'd seen her grandparents and family, but they were in caskets and looked more like wax figures than real people. The man lying next to her…he had a look of surprise and pain on his face. Not to mention she'd never seen so much blood before. Her stomach heaved, and Lucy swore she'd never eat blackberries again.

Simon. How was it possible to be in a relationship with someone and know so little about who they truly were on the inside? What an idiot she was to land in such a big mess. A tear landed on the tip of her nose. First things first. Find a phone and warn her sisters. Then get on the next plane home. Not in a million years would she ever set foot out of North Carolina again.

Pain pierced her heart. Would she make it home only to plan the funerals of her sisters? Deep down, she worried she was too late. One thing about Simon, he always finished what he started. The pain shredding her body made Lucy trip, landing on her knees. A cry of pain escaped her battered throat. Her arm was bleeding. The pain she'd felt earlier? One of those men had actually cut her. They were taking this living in another time stuff way too seriously. As she stood, a ripping sound filled the air. A bloody knee poked through the dress. On the bright side, now she could run.

Torches lit the stairway as she frantically made her way down. Limp, step, limp, step. She stopped, kicked off the remaining sparkly shoe and fled down the stone steps. At the bottom she came to another door. Odd—she didn't remember taking a door up to the second floor. Leaning against it with her shoulder, she shrieked when someone yanked her backward into a wall. Desperately sucking in air, she grabbed the forearm across her chest. The owner of said arm spun her around.

Mr. Green Eyes. He towered over her, yelling and shaking her shoes in front of her. Lucy couldn't understand a single word. It was like French but not. Some kind of whack-a-doodle English? Her confusion must have shown, for he switched to a version of English she could understand.

"Demoiselle, why did you murder my man? Who sent you?" He glared down at her and she froze, hoping the apex predator would pass by if she pretended to be invisible. No such luck.

The man curled his lip. "How did you end Alan?" Green eyes darkened. "A mere wench. Where is your companion? I will run him through. And you will die next to him."

"Die! I didn't kill anyone. When I woke, he was lying next to me on the ground. I don't know what happened."

The man sneered at her. "You are covered in his blood. Yet you proclaim your innocence? Do you take me for a fool?"

Lucy threw up her hands in exasperation. "I was trying to tell those men. Simon tried to kill me, and when I woke up, he was gone and…and…ugh!"

She couldn't help it. The strain of the past night and this morning was too much. Lucy couldn't hold it together for another second. She sobbed and pounded on the man's chest as he held her. In that flash of insight you sometimes get in moments of extreme emotion, Lucy knew deep in her bones that something was terribly, horribly, dreadfully wrong. She wasn't in Kansas anymore. If she were in Vegas, she'd bet every cent to her name—she wasn't in the twenty-first century anymore.

Chapter Four

Late Summer, 1307 - Blackford Castle, England

William Brandon, formerly the son of the earl of Ravenswing, currently the lord of Blackford Castle, scowled down at the sobbing female in his arms and cursed heartily. He was finding it difficult to believe this slip of a girl had killed his guard, no matter what the men thought.

What else would go wrong this day? Three days had passed since he rode across the drawbridge to his new estate. Three days of frustration and complaints from his childhood friend turned steward, Clement.

William wanted nothing more than to go back to his chamber and pretend this day never dawned. But that would not do. He needed to face this latest problem, hopefully the last in a long string of miserable events. The garrison knights thought the woman dead until she started to struggle under the body of Alan. A frown crossed his face. William wondered if his guard was protecting the girl.

Some unknown person had savagely beaten the wench. The marks on her face and ivory throat sent a bolt of anger coursing through his body. If he found who dared to strike her, William would end the man responsible where he stood. Never would he allow a man to ill-use a woman. Nothing explained why the men had not seen the girl arrive.

The white gown would have been visible in the storm. How did she make it all the way to the battlements unchallenged? And what was the nonsense she'd spewed? He hadn't listened, he'd been so shocked by her appearance. There had been rumors of secret passages in his home, at which he had scoffed. Mayhap 'twas time to investigate. He would have plenty of time now.

He absently patted the lady's shoulder. Her sobbing gave way to small noises like those of a wounded animal. Why was the alarm not raised? One of the men should have found his fallen guard and the girl whilst going about his duties. So many unanswered questions made his head ache.

William felt every day of his score-and-five years of age pondering the ways she could have come to be in his home. Why did someone try to murder her? Was she a threat? Many nobles were unhappy he'd been awarded Blackford. Mayhap they were plotting against him. He swore and set his bundle on her feet, patting her full arse.

The lass had courage to match her beauty. He rubbed his stomach, the corner of his mouth quirking up. Her form was good, though the execution fell short. Fortunate she didn't break her thumb. He would teach her to keep her thumb on the outside of her fist the next time she tried to throttle someone.

One of the guards, wearing his fear on his face like a mask, interrupted his reverie, presenting him with the shoes William had dropped. They were blue, encrusted with gems and shone brilliantly in the sunlight. The man crossed himself. "She's a witch come to steal our manhood and take our souls to the devil. She killed Alan with her foul incantations."

William resisted the urge to chuckle and settled instead for rolling his eyes. "Then why does she cower at my feet? Not a very powerful witch."

The horrorstruck look on the man's face made William choke back laughter. He quickly sobered. Witchcraft was nothing to jest about. He had witnessed many places and strange doings, but would wager on his best horse this girl was no witch.

"Don't be daft, man. The lady is not a witch." He crossed his fingers behind his back and looked the guard square in the face. "Look at her. Witches are ugly old hags, with warts and long noses. Does she look like a witch to you?"

The man peered closer, and William resisted the urge to shout and startle him. The guard scratched his nose and said rather dubiously, "I suppose not, but then how did she come to kill Alan? She should die, my lord."

"Alan was thrice her size. She could not have murdered him." William held up a hand, thinking. "Take the men and search the castle, grounds and the cove. She must have had assistance." She'd spoken strangely and babbled about someone named Simon. Her accomplice?

The guard looked her over. "Is she one of Clement's wenches?"

"Look at her, man, does she look like a whore?" William stared at the girl, who was trying to curl into a ball at his feet. Small sobs occasionally escaped as she rocked back and forth. Other than the injuries he could see, she had the skin of a wee babe. The dress and shoes were strange but finely wrought. So many gems on her shoes, William would wager she was wealthy and thus a lady. Though why was she alone without escort?

The guard scratched his arse. "She looks like a lady."

"Begone."

The guard scurried away, calling to the men. William would have to deal with Clement, his friend since childhood. William had not realized how much his friend changed whilst William was away fighting. He was also a third son. Now fallen on hard times since the family fell into disfavor with the king.

Being stripped of title and lands would send any man to drink and wenching. From what William remembered, Clement had a slovenly character even as a boy. Only now was it wearing on William's patience. He was growing old. Dealing with Clement would wait. After all, he couldn't stand around gaping at the woman like a simpleton all day.

Was it too much to ask to come home after fighting for so many years and want to be left in peace? Far away from the rumors that followed him like a curse. He'd been with his king, Edward I, at the battle of Falkirk. Witnessed firsthand the fall of William Wallace. Continued to fight, and was present when Edward passed recently during the campaign against Robert the Bruce, now King of Scotland.

He snorted. Let the Scots keep their bloody country. Now there was a new king, Edward II. A weak king. William had made his way home titled and richer.

Only to find his closest friend, who'd been left in charge of the castle, hadn't done anything other than eat, drink and wench during the years William was away fighting.

Most of the walls were falling down, the floors so thick with refuse and muck that he slipped and fell on his backside when he made his grand entrance. Pride bruised more than anything, he almost heaved his guts at the unholy stench pervading his home. Cook hadn't provided an edible meal since his return. The stables were in shambles, the cows and sheep long ago stolen, and he'd found three hens in his bedchamber. Asleep in his bed.

He'd always known Clement ran to idleness, but how could he have let matters fall into such disrepair? William was awarded Blackford after he'd saved his king during battle. Aching from his injuries and unable to leave, he'd sent a missive asking Clement to manage the estate until the fighting ended. He would have been better off leaving it undefended.

And now he had a wench to contend with. His men swore they hadn't snuck her into the keep, and when he looked closely, she didn't look like a whore or peasant girl from the village, even if she was dressed like one, with an abundance of golden skin showing.

The dress was white and molded to her shapely form. Her skin the color of a ripe peach, unblemished and unmarked. He peered down at the female in question. Her skin was soft as a babe and smelled like a summer day. Her face was pleasing, with full pink lips and dark lashes, hair the brown of his favorite horse.

What color were her eyes? The fact he'd been staring at her overlong told him he'd not been in the company of a lady in a long time. There was something strange afoot here. The material of the dress was finer than any he'd seen, even in France. He squinted in the dim corridor and shrugged.

How would he know what fashionable ladies wore? Fashion. He never paid attention. As long as he had clothes on his back, he was content to let others such as Clement look the peacock.

Who was she? Clearly the girl didn't speak the language. Whilst he understood the meaning, the accent was the slow drawl more of a commoner than a highborn lady. Though he had never heard the king's English spoken in such a manner or with such inflection. A chuckle escaped as he rubbed his stomach again. The wench possessed a strong arm.

A finger jabbed him in the side. "Heard you found a lass. I'll take her."

"She isn't a horse to be bought and sold, Clement. Look at her —she's of highborn stock. Though how she ended up on my battlements is beyond my understanding."

The female in question had her ears covered with her hands and was softly humming to herself. Clement stared down at the wench, a look of lust filling his face. This wouldn't do.

"Move." William shoved at his steward. They couldn't very well stand in the corridor blocking the way all day. "The wench needs tending to."

"You swore a woman would never reside under your roof again. She is a witch. Burn her."

"No burnings. She is no witch." Leave it to Clement to bring up the one part of his life he never wanted to remember. William bared his teeth and elbowed his steward out of the way.

"Damnable chivalry," he grumbled as he scooped the lass up into his arms. She let out a shriek.

"Silence," he roared. He'd had enough disorder for the day. William felt the back of her head. There was a large bump, and likely it would pain her with a fearsome ache. She bore a minor cut on her forearm and stomach. Other than that, she didn't seem to have any broken bones, despite the rent in her dress. He cast a critical eye over his burden, noting the dress looked to be ruined after being out in the rain all night. It was more gray than white, and spattered with blood, mud and other muck he'd rather not think about.

His guest looked up at him through dark lashes and eyes as gray as a winter sky. She mumbled something unintelligible then fell silent. He had much to see to without a bloody woman to worry over. Shifting her weight, he felt the bare skin of her legs as he placed one arm more firmly under her knees. They were smooth as silk. Not like other women he'd bedded with furry legs to match his own.

What would it be like to bed a woman who was slippery as a seal? Not that he'd do anything of the sort with this woman, it was simply idle speculation. For Clement was correct. William allowed his men to frequent the wenches in the village. But women were not to reside under his roof. After Georgina, he'd never trust another woman again. Bed them but never love them.

He shifted the weight in his arms. Whatever her circumstances, he'd see her fed and on her way with one of his men to see her safe on the morrow. For he knew she had not killed his guard. He would puzzle out her identity and how she came to be in his home without escort later. For he did not want her under his roof any longer than need be.

An overlarge group gathered as he entered the hall. William raised his head and met the eye of every servant and warrior.

"The woman is under my protection." Not a soul would gainsay him. He had matters to attend to, matters that did not include a lost lady. William planned to remain without a shrewish wife who would plague him the rest of his days. He wanted to be left alone to forget the horrors he had witnessed. Here at Blackford, no one would whisper behind his back. Women were no longer welcome in his life.

A string of curses left his lips as he carried her through the hall and up the stairs. Startled men scurried out of his way. The wench took one look around his hall and fell senseless. He supposed that bespoke volumes regarding the state of his household.

"Bring wine and bread."

Without waiting to see who obeyed, he took the stairs two at a time and paused on the threshold. Other than his and Clement's rooms, the rest of the hall was still in a state of filth and disrepair. A hearty sigh left his lips, and with another muttered curse, he kicked the door open to his own chamber.

Removed from his own bed by a woman. He should lock her in

one of the filthy rooms with a guard, though truly he would not believe she'd had a hand in the death of his guard. He was growing soft. William should put her in the stables. Though they weren't much different from the rest of Blackford in terms of order and cleanliness. One stall for his own horse was clean, and for the rest he'd commandeered three small boys to work in the stables, clearing out the refuse.

With a withering glare at the senseless maid in his bed, William gave up pondering questions he had no answer to. On the morrow he would have answers before sending her away. No matter how fetching she be. He'd been through muck and blood up to his elbows. How hard could it be to manage a slip of a girl?

William cast a baleful eye over her, muttering as he took his leave. Halfway down the corridor he bellowed, "Thomas, John!" The men appeared breathless in front of him.

"Guard the wench. One of you fetch food from the kitchens." Unease slithered around his stomach as if he'd swallowed live eels.

Chapter Five

Lucy jerked awake. "Simon, I had the worst nightmare."

The covers fell off as she sat up with a groan. It was freezing in here. What she wouldn't give for the blistering heat of a day at the beach right about now. She shivered again, looking around the room. Nothing made any sense. The bed was the same yet different. The mattress felt lumpy, the sheets like old linen. The blankets wool and velvet. Come to think of it, the room was different too. There were lush tapestries on the walls, a fire in the fireplace, papers on the desk and a pair of boots next to a chest. The room looked lived in, not abandoned and dusty as she'd remembered from last night.

And why was she still in the wedding gown? Had she gone swimming in the sea in the beautiful dress and ruined it? Given the monster headache, maybe she'd drunk an entire bottle of champagne herself? Lucy sniffed. Leaned down to the dress and sniffed again. Ugh. She smelled too awful for this to be a dream.

And then like a freight train missing a curve and derailing, everything came rushing back. Her subconscious decided at that moment to wake up and start yelling. *The drugged champagne. Simon yammering on about some stupid curse, and let's not forget him tricking you into actually marrying him and then trying to kill you.*

How very wrong she'd been. Another mistake. This one worse than all the ones before. How could she have been so stupid? She had the worst taste in the history of the world when it came to falling for the wrong guy. Oh no, she was married to him. No, no, no. Her wedding was supposed to be special, a happy occasion, not something she wanted to forget ever happened.

And what did he mean, she was descended from the Brandon line but Charlotte and Melinda weren't? He'd never loved her. Only wanted her because of some ridiculously wrong family tree. What hurt even more? He thought she was mousy and common. Insults of the past came screaming back, and she was five again, hiding in the dusty stacks of the library at school, crying her eyes out.

Oh God, her sisters. What time was it? She searched the bed for her phone, coming up empty. Was she too late—were they already dead? Her feet hit a soft rug as Lucy frantically looked under the bed and in every corner of the room for her phone. A jumbled image of the phone flying over the wall and crashing on the rocks below filled her mind.

After what seemed like hours, she slumped in the chair in front of the desk unseeing, replaying the horrible events of last night over and over again. A vague impression of someone watching over her last night flitted through her mind and was gone as quick as a hummingbird.

The sound of clanging steel dragged her from mentally yelling at herself for the hundredth time. On tiptoe, she peered out of the window and staggered back, black spots dancing in front of her eyes. They were back. The re-enactors had taken over the entire castle. Did Simon rent the place out? She needed a phone to call her sisters. Surely one of those crazy guys had one stashed in his tights.

The dead guy. How could she be so selfish as to forget about him? The room tilted, her stomach heaved and Lucy pictured the guy on the ground in a pool of blood. Swallowing, she opened her eyes and looked outside again. Not a single police car or ambulance. Maybe they'd been and gone? But wouldn't they want to talk to her?

The heavy door looked new. Lucy pulled it open and jumped back. A boy was leaning against the wall.

"My lady? May I be of assistance? I am Albin." He gave a small bow. She peered at him. He looked young, though it was hard to tell in the gloom. Albin was dressed like the others in some sort of tunic and hose. At least he didn't pretend not to speak English. She peered up and down the corridor.

"I need to go outside, but first I need the bathroom." And with that, she pushed past him and stomped down the corridor.

"A bathroom?" He whimpered.

Seriously. This was taking the acting thing a bit far. Ignoring him, Lucy continued to explore, wishing her head would clear.

The boy looked about ten or eleven, and followed behind her, babbling the entire way. "Lady, stop. I'm to guard you. My lord won't be pleased."

"Your lord can stuff it. I've had enough of this nonsense. Take me to the man in charge."

The boy gulped, and she felt like a brat.

"Everything will be fine, you'll see." She patted his sleeve and smiled when he blushed. Lucy came down the stairs feeling a bit woozy and icky. She desperately needed to brush her teeth. The tiny room that she thought was a bathroom was nothing more than a hole in a stone seat with what looked like hay in a bucket.

The smell told her it was some kind of primitive outhouse. Or was it an in-house, since it was inside? There wasn't a shower to be found. She knew. She'd checked every door. No mirror, either. Her throat burned and her face throbbed in time with her headache, but considering she'd escaped with her life, she wasn't going to complain.

The stairs too seemed somehow different. Less worn, newer. Then again, it was night and she'd been drugged, so she probably wasn't clear on several things.

Except for one—she was now married to Simon. At least until she could get it annulled. He'd committed fraud, tricked her. She would see him in jail if it was the last thing she did.

Right. She'd have been better off marrying one of the cute cows in the field outside. Her husband. Nope. Make that her soon-to-be ex-husband. It would be the quickest marriage and divorce ever. Even shorter than some of the celebrities she loved to read about.

There had to be some crazy explanation for what was happening to her. Or she'd had one hell of a hallucination or some kind of bad drug trip. Either way, it was time to get answers. There was no way she'd fallen through time. Nope. That only happened in books and movies. Not in real life.

She tripped and fell over the last step, landing in a heap on the floor. The dress ripped again and she felt like crying. What if her sisters were dead? There had to be time to warn them. Nothing else was acceptable.

The boy made a sound of distress. "Forgive me, lady."

As the re-enactors in the hall moved around her, Lucy's mouth fell open. She shut it just as fast and pinched her nose with her fingers before she threw up. The smell. It was like a garbage dump on a hot summer day overlaid with body odor, animal odor and—she wrinkled her nose, breathing shallowly through her mouth—something dead.

"Ewww, this is disgusting."

The scene before her was a bit too authentic for her tastes.

There were a few tapestries on the wall, and enormous fireplaces flanked the room set into the wall. She squinted, noticing the stone hearths carved with scenes of animals. A man sat back and critically looked over the carving he was working on. There were a few chairs in front of the hearth, looking like a nice spot to curl up with a book.

Overall, the hall seemed in better condition than she'd thought last night—well, except for the smell. She would have remembered such a dreadful stench. People came and went, all dressed in period clothing. Forget the re-enactors. Maybe they were filming a movie.

A tiny voice in her head whispered again she was no longer in the twenty-first century, but Lucy was having none of that nonsense. As Aunt Mildred used to say, no sense borrowing trouble.

The boy caught up to her and took her arm. He sighed, a long-suffering sigh. "This way, lady."

Were his teeth chattering? What on earth was he so afraid of?

The heavy doors to outside and fresh air beckoned, and Lucy followed her nose. Barefoot, wearing a rumpled wedding dress, with half her hair hanging down her back, she looked around and hoped she hadn't stepped into the middle of filming and ruined the shot. No one yelled "cut," so she followed the sounds around the corner and stopped, blinking at the sight.

"Albin?"

The boy took a firm grip on her arm. "Not to worry, lady, I won't let you fall again."

"It's Lucy. My name is Lucy."

Some of the walls were falling down, and the stables looked half-finished. A scraggly garden in one corner, a few ramshackle buildings along one wall and a chapel also awaited repair.

The scene in front of her was sheer chaos. Men fought with swords. It didn't look like playacting. They looked deadly serious. The boy led the way and she followed, whipping her head back and forth, trying to take everything in.

"Hello, I need a phone." Lucy coughed and covered her mouth to keep the dust out. Swords clanged, men grunted and she smelled horses and sweat. No one paid any attention to her. It was certainly a masculine scene. Though where were the cameras? The director? Not a movie-type person to be seen. Okay, so not a movie.

Re-enactors. A man landed at her feet with a grunt, wiped blood from his mouth, swore and slashed up at his attacker. Lucy jumped back. They were awfully authentic. She touched a hand to her bandaged forearm. Hadn't she been cut last night? While she was biting her lower lip trying to come up with a plausible solution to the chaos in front of her, *he* stalked toward her.

"Albin. I told you to guard the lady. What is she doing in the lists?"

It was the man from her bad acid trip, as she was now calling it. But hallucinations went away when you woke up. Could she still be tripping? She wished she'd read more about drugs, but she'd never tried anything stronger than pot, and it was only the one time. It made her feel nauseated and icky, and after that it was a couple glasses of wine and she was tipsy as a cat on catnip.

The boy stuttered and turned pale. "She's powerful quick, my lord."

"Off with you. I'll see to the wench."

The man nearing them was sexy and scary at the same time, which, according to her new code, meant he was bad news. There was a scar at the corner of his nose that gave him a rakish pirate look. Busy eyeing him, she didn't hear him at first.

"Demoiselle?" He scowled.

She had no clue what the rest of the words meant.

"Sorry, I don't speak French. That is what you're speaking, right? Do y'all speak English?" Great. Her accent always came out when she was nervous. Now she probably sounded like some ditzy

Southern belle.

"I need to borrow your phone. It's an emergency. I have to call my sisters. And the police."

"You require aid, my lady?" The man with the greenest eyes she'd ever seen cocked an eyebrow.

"Cut the act. This is serious. Your phone. Now. And what's with all the 'my lady' stuff? My name is Lucy."

"Lady, you have a bump on your head and are not yourself. Does your throat and face pain you? I dressed the wound on your arm, so it should not putrefy." He handed her some kind of leather-looking bottle. "I know not this word 'phone.' If you keep standing there gaping, my lady, you may find yourself in danger. Sit on the bench and wait."

"It's Lucy. Just Lucy." How bossy! The infuriating man looked down his crooked nose at her and crossed massive arms over his chest. What, was he going to start tapping his foot if she didn't move?

"Arf. Arf. Fine. And I wasn't staring. I've just never seen re-enactor knights before. You're very authentic. Did you travel here from France"—she gestured to the men around them—"to practice? Will there be a joust and tournament?" Lucy opened the bottle and drank, sputtering at the taste.

The blow on her back almost sent her to her knees. "Better?" The man peered at her like she was some kind of interesting bug pinned to a board.

"My men and I train daily. Blackford is my home. Gifted to me for service to my king." He rubbed his shoulder. "We hold no tournament. I want no visitors. Only to be left alone."

Meaning he didn't want her around. Lucy didn't want to be here anyway. She needed to go home. She sent up a prayer. *Please don't let Charlotte and Melinda be dead.* She blinked back the tear that threatened to fall and made her way over to a stone bench set against a wall, dragging the tattered gown as she walked.

How could he not know the word for phone? Talk about taking this historic thing to silly levels. And why couldn't she see the cottage? Lucy leaned back and looked around. Where was the road? The castle looked new. No longer a ruin.

No longer a ruin.

The men. The people around her. The language. Her brain kept screaming the truth at her, but she'd refused to listen. There was only one explanation that made sense.

She had fallen.

Through time. But to when?

All of a sudden, she put her head between her knees. "Please, don't let me faint."

Tiny yellow and green spots danced in front of her eyes. A low buzzing filled her ears, and for the first time in her twenty-four years, she thought she might be having a heart attack—or was it a panic attack?

"My lady, do you require aid?"

As if she had conjured him, the bossy man knelt before her, looking at her with concern in his eyes.

"I think I'm having a heart attack."

"You are under attack?" He pursed his lips. "I see no one wishing you ill."

"Panic attack." Pant. Blink. Count to five and breathe. The primitive part of her brain ignored the emotional crazy going on and took a moment to admire the man in front of her. Lucy swallowed as her mouth filled with saliva.

This guy was built like a brick wall. Those broad shoulders, narrow waist, strong legs. This was not a body made in the gym but one made with serious hard work—right, like swinging and hacking away at enemies with the wicked-looking sword hanging from his hip.

One of the other men with a sword scowled down at her. "She speaks the vulgar tongue of the lower classes. Send her away."

"Back to the lists. I shall aid this lady." The man stomped away and then Mr. Green Eyes touched her arm.

"My lady?"

The softly spoken word drew her attention. "The feeling is passing. I think I'm okay. At least now I know why no one has a phone. And this might explain why I can't find the rat extraordinaire, Simon."

He looked at her as if she was an escapee from an asylum. "You are unwell. Albin will see you to your chamber."

"No," she whispered to herself. "I have no way to warn them." She clutched at his tunic. "Don't you understand? I'm too late. They're dead. Because of me."

And without warning, Lucy threw up all over his boots.

Chapter Six

The world continued to spin. Lucy heaved a few more times before risking a look at the man in front of her. She felt weightless, boneless, as if she'd died and was floating to heaven.

A piece of fabric was thrust into her face.

"I threw up on your boots." She wiped her face, cheeks flaming. "I'm so sorry."

She must have looked panicked, because the man gently placed her beside him on the stone bench. Grateful, she leaned in to him, inhaling sweat, wool and horse.

"Allow me to introduce myself. I am Lord Blackford. William. What is your name, my lady?"

Her subconscious butted in again. *You're in a hospital in a coma, having a dream.*

Shut up, she told herself. *I am not.* He was obviously an ancestor of Simon's with the Lord Blackford stuff. Which meant he was no good. But shouldn't his last name be Grey? Though she'd always liked the name William. It was a strong, solid name. Would he help her when he knew her story? Her mind was going in fifty different directions at once.

"Lady? Your name?"

"Lucy Merriweather. I don't suppose you could tell me what year it is?"

William spent a restless night slumped in a damned uncomfortable chair watching Lucy sleep. He'd left before dawn to take his frustration out in the lists. No one knew any more about her. His men found no signs of any traveling party. No sign of a struggle. It was as if the wench appeared out of the sky and landed in his castle.

And then she was ill on his boots. He cast a critical eye over his unwanted guest. As unpleasant a thought as it was, William could see no way to be rid of the wench. Damnable chivalry. The lass couldn't keep wandering around in a tattered, bloodstained dress. She was starting to smell, her hair looked as if she'd spent a night in his stables and her feet were filthy. Yet her face was pleasing, her body made of curves a man could sink himself into and her eyes, he could stare into them all day. No. He shook his head. He would not be bewitched by another lying female.

He looked her up and down and answered the girl's odd question. "The Year of Our Lord 1307."

"Perchance the wench is feebleminded and should be sent away to a convent."

Lucy lunged for Simon. "You. How dare you drug me, trick me into marrying you for real and then try to kill me. I'll have you thrown in jail." She slapped him hard across the face, gratified to hear the smack echo across the courtyard. "My sisters better be okay, you horrible pig!"

Simon reached out to grab her. "How dare this witch strike me? I'll kill her where she stands."

"Enough," William bellowed, quieting them both. He grabbed Lucy and glared at Simon. "We do not kill women."

She was shaking. "I seem to have made a mistake." The man looked so much like Simon it was uncanny, but, looking closer, she could see small differences. Horrified, she looked at the man.

"You look exactly like Simon. I'm sorry I hit you."

The man said something that didn't sound very complimentary before William frowned at him.

"Begone, Clement, and leave the wench to me. I'll see you in the solar momentarily."

Lucy was busy sucking in shallow breaths of air. The walls of the courtyard seemed to pulse in time to the screech of metal on metal. Her stomach protested, but thankfully nothing else came up.

She'd fallen through time over seven hundred years. How was it possible? She was stupid to have believed in Simon. Stupid for ignoring the warnings in her head. A wet spot appeared on her hand. The raindrops ran down the side of her hand and made a dark mark on the filthy white dress. Hysterical laughter bubbled up.

"I've ruined my dress and I don't have any shoes." The shock must be wearing off just in time for her situation to sink in. 1307. Alone. Simon was still back in her time. And she was separated from her sisters by not only an ocean but over seven hundred years. With no way to go back in time to warn them.

Lucy jumped up and ran for the hall. If she could get back to the battlements, she could go home.

A string of angry French followed her. She risked a quick look over her shoulder. William was following her while keeping his men back. He made no move to stop her.

She raced up the stairs, panting and seeing spots. The door opened with a creak and there was light. Where was the bench? Heedless of the cold stone on her feet, Lucy passed by one bench and then the next. As she came to the third, she saw something sparkling in the sun. Lucy knelt down, reached in the corner and picked up a crystal that must have fallen off her shoes as another seam in the dress gave way.

What did she need to do? First, she closed her eyes and pictured home. The sound of a throat clearing broke her concentration, and she opened her eyes to see William standing a few feet away, arms crossed over his chest, watching her with an inscrutable expression on his face. The man would make an excellent poker player.

She tried sitting on the bench and picturing the castle as it had been. A ruin, nighttime, thunder and lightning and rain. Lucy counted to fifty and opened her eyes.

"Damn it to hell." There was no rusty-looking spot anywhere near the bench. Somehow she thought she'd touched that spot and felt a jolt, but it could have been the whole getting struck by lightning thing. So maybe she really was in a coma in the hospital. In that case, she needed to wake up. Now. With a vicious twist, she pinched the soft skin below her nonexistent bicep.

"Ow!" Nope, she was awake and present in this circle of hell.

William blinked but made no move toward her. She noted he motioned to the curious guards to stay back.

Arm smarting, she jumped up. "Hmmm…well, it can't hurt."

Closing her eyes, she whispered the words from *The Wizard of Oz*. It worked for Dorothy, so it should work for her.

"There's no place like home, there's no place like home, there's no place like home." Lucy didn't want to open her eyes, so instead she kept them closed tight and listened. No thunder, but she heard rain—and the sound of swords.

A tear fell. Then another, and before she knew it, William was patting her on the back hard enough to make her fall off the bench. He pulled her down next to him. Another piece of cloth was thrust at her. This huge, ferocious-looking man petted her hair and murmured soft words to her. She didn't understand most of the words but swore one of them was "horse."

"My sisters are most likely dead." She looked up at him through a film of tears. "Why does whatshisname look exactly like Simon?"

William watched in fascination as the girl engaged in strange doings. His fascination quickly turned to horror as her eyes began to leak. He grumbled under his breath, hoping she wouldn't heave her guts on his person again. Though he was doubtful she had anything left in her.

Womanly tears made him feel helpless, and William Brandon was never helpless. Fearsome, mayhap. Frowning severely, he hauled her down and onto his lap, hoping she would cease her blubbering. Not knowing how to comfort the woman, he spoke low words to her like he did to a frightened horse. The lady, Lucy, continued to leak, so he patted her shoulder and let her cry.

She blew her nose and wiped her eyes, and he was glad he had

listened to his mother and always carried two cloths with him.
Saints help him if she started leaking again. The lady must be
feebleminded to ask him for the year.

Womanly matters finished, William took her hand and drew it
through the crook of his elbow. "Time in the lists usually soothes
my temper."

He led Lucy back down the stairs, through his hall and back out
to the lists. Several of his knights paused to glance their way before
hastily averting their eyes from William's frown.

He led her over to a bench and saw her seated.

"Why do y'all have a dog on your shields? Why not a lion or a
bear?"

She was peering at him, her nose wrinkled up as if she found
his herald distasteful.

He stiffened. "'Tis no dog, lady, but a hellhound. Legend says
one protected the castle when it was in danger in 1129, and has
been our herald ever since."

"Oh. That explains the snarling and red eyes. Whatever. It looks
like a dog with rabies to me."

She was a saucy wench. William left her sitting on the bench and
made his way back to the men.

A noise drew his attention. When he turned, it was to see a
huge raven perched on the edge of the bench. The bird looked him
over, turned its head to watch his men and then turned to Lucy. It
made a soft sound, and she spoke to the creature.

Men mumbled and crossed themselves. William was a learned
man, so he resisted the urge, barely. After a few minutes, the bird
cawed and flew away.

"My lord, she is a witch."

Another knight leaned on his sword. "She was communing with
the creature."

"Unwholesome doings. We must drown her in the sea," chimed

a third knight.

His garrison knights' reactions bespoke dire tidings. It would not do for them to go around spreading rumors of a witch at Blackford Castle. The new king would likely take the castle and all its lands.

William cast a baleful eye over his men. "Womanly prattle, the lot of you. Now draw your blades. I will grind each man into the dirt one by one. Who is first?"

Chapter Seven

William woke in the morning, annoyed. He had given up his chamber to the wench and was currently sleeping in a filthy chamber with tattered bed coverings. Not for the first time, he wondered if Edward thought to make a jest by rewarding him with Blackford. No, his king, God rest his soul, was never one to jest. The banging on his door did little to improve his mood.

"My lord, come quickly—there are men at the gates asking for you."

Taking the stairs two at a time, he made his way out of the castle to the portcullis.

"Let them pass."

Three men stood before him. Men he had fought beside, bled with—most importantly, men he trusted.

"Heard Edward had awarded you a castle. Thought we'd come take a look for ourselves." The man standing before him was a fearsome warrior.

William clapped him on the shoulder. "Welcome." He looked to the other two men, nodded and gestured for them to follow.

"The walls are falling down, the stables in disrepair, my halls reek with foul odors and the food is dreadful. If these things don't scare you off, be welcome in my hall."

The three men laughed. "We come to serve you, my lord."

"No, I'm still William to you. No longer fighting as mercenaries?"

One of the others spoke up. "Heard you were awarded Blackford for saving the old king's life. Thought you could use our blades at your side."

The frustration William had felt since he arrived at Blackford abated upon seeing the warriors. Men he had fought alongside many times over the years. For as much as it pained him, he was no longer sure he trusted Clement. In fact, he wondered if he'd ever trusted the man he called friend growing up.

William showed the men to the garrison. It was one of the few buildings in decent repair. "You'll have a roof over your heads. The masons have begun work."

Then he went to find Lucy. First he stopped in the kitchen.

"Have hot water and the bathing tub filled for the lady."

Without waiting to see if he was obeyed, William turned and stalked out of the kitchens. He hesitated at the door to his chamber. It galled him to knock on his own door. Lucy opened the door looking as if she'd slept in the dreadful gown.

"A good morrow to you, my lady."

Lucy looked up at him. "Please call me Lucy."

He gestured to her dress. "I will procure clothing for you today. In the meantime, I thought you might enjoy a bath."

"Oh, yes please. That would be delightful. I smell like a skunk that's been run over three times."

Shaking his head at her odd speech, William led her down the stairs through the kitchens and into a small room.

"I didn't even have water to wash my face, so thank you for the bath."

Was the wench daft?

"Did you not see the pipe for water in the chamber? Blackford may be falling apart; however, the pipe bringing cold water to the chamber is a most recent invention." The girl had probably never seen water running out of a wall before.

There was a knock at the door. "Enter."

Three young boys hurried into the chamber and proceeded to fill the bathing tub whilst casting nervous looks at Lucy. He needed to ensure no rumors of witchcraft spread about his guest.

Her stomach rumbled. William turned his head. When was the last time she had eaten? His own stomach sent up a protest, making him wonder when he'd last broken his fast. A new cook was of great import.

"I do not have many servants."

She looked at him with gray eyes the color of the ocean outside after a storm. And William was reminded why he wanted no women in his hall. She looked nothing like Georgina, but all women were treacherous. He would be on his guard.

"Why not? I'd think a castle this big would need a lot of help. I had a housekeeper, and my house was tiny compared to this place."

She spoke in a strange manner, enough so William had difficulty following her speech.

He stiffened. "I am recently returned from fighting for my king. Most of the servants left before I arrived."

"Okay." She wandered around the room, looking at the hearth and bathing tub as if she had never seen such things before. Many did not bathe. William grew up bathing and preferred it to smelling foul.

"Bring the lady something to eat." William sent the boys on

their way and turned to face Lucy. "I'm afraid the cook produces less-than-palatable food. Until I find someone else, it will have to do."

"What I wouldn't give for a pizza and a glass of sweet tea."

"You have a strange manner of speaking, my lady." He wondered again where she was from and what she was doing in his hall.

"Well, so do you, buster."

He would ponder this "buster" later. With a look over his shoulder, William opened the door. "I have sent for clothing from the village for you to wear, my lady."

The men left, shutting the door behind them. Lucy couldn't get out of the tattered, soiled and horribly smelly dress fast enough. There was no way the dress would come clean. Such an expensive dress reduced to rags. The thought of the amount of money thrown out the window made her cringe. While it was the dream dress she'd posted on her wedding board, Lucy never would have spent so much on a dress she'd only wear once. Instead, she'd rather put the money toward a cottage on the beach.

It was colder inside the castle than outside. William told her the year, though she hadn't thought to ask the month and day. Wouldn't it be the same month? Did it matter? By the temperature outside, it must still be summer.

Strange to have fires burning inside in the fireplaces when it was warm outside. The room he'd taken her to was off the large kitchen. Not a tapestry or painted wall in sight; nothing but cold stone. When she laid a hand on the stone, she felt the damp. It smelled faintly of the ocean outside.

One man handed her some kind of rough towel and a lump of what she assumed was soap before he shut the door. Sniffing it, she wrinkled her nose then decided it likely smelled better than she did. She reeked.

Steam rose off the water. Lucy stuck a finger in to test the temperature. It was blissfully hot, and she climbed in with a sigh. As she drew her knees up and sank down into the bath, she thought about the events of the past several days. You couldn't make this kind of story up. She'd gone through every explanation and was left with the fact she was in the past.

Not sure how long it would take her to find a way back home to her own time, Lucy decided she'd best dig into her brain for what she knew of this time. Knowledge was power, no matter what time period you found yourself in.

William had confirmed the date, and as she scrubbed the dirt and grime off her body, she thought about what she knew of the time. During high school she paid enough attention to pass history. In college she took the basics required for her business degree. This was one of those times she wished she'd grown up in Europe and had a more detailed knowledge of history.

Lucy worked on washing her long, matted hair while she reviewed what she did know. Based on the date, it was Norman French that William and his men were speaking. No wonder it sounded so strange to her ears. Then again, she was pretty certain they'd never heard a Southern accent like hers either.

Everyone knew about William Wallace thanks to *Braveheart*. He'd died two years ago, and Edward was king. Had Edward I died yet? If not, he'd be dead soon—wasn't it July when he died? His son would take the throne. Crap on toast, when was the black plague? She racked her brain—maybe mid-thirteen hundreds? Lucy shuddered in the wooden tub despite the warmth. She did not want to be stuck here and live through such a horrific epidemic.

So England and Scotland were feuding. Robert the Bruce hadn't beaten Edward II at Bannockburn yet. Did she know anything else? Edward II would be murdered. Bad weather and famine. Not a good time to be stuck in the past. Lucy searched her mind for any fragment of history mentioning Blackford Castle. All she came up with was what Simon had told her.

She sat up in the tub sloshing water over the side onto the stone floor. He'd said his ancestor took the castle by force from a traitor in…1307. This year. Who was the ancestor? This time she stood up. It was the man she'd mistaken for Simon. Clement was his name.

He had to be the one, right? Though a lot could happen over several months in medieval England. Did she warn William? What would she say? *Hi, I'm not a witch, I'm from the future, and your friend Clement is going to make you a traitor and take your castle?*

Right. He'd have the fire going and her at the stake before she could say "broomstick" three times fast.

No, she'd do what she did whenever she was in an unfamiliar situation. Keep her mouth shut and watch. Learn. Then she would figure out what to do. How to get back home to face whatever awaited.

As she air-dried by the fire, Lucy waited. Still no one came. The gown lay on the floor, a wrinkled mess. What could it hurt? She picked up the gown and dunked it in the tub. Doing her best to wash it out with the small sliver of soap left, she made a face as the water turned gray. Yuck.

Once she'd wrung out the water as best she could, Lucy laid the dress by the fire to dry. Then she sat down on a stool next to the fire, covered herself with the small piece of fabric that passed for a towel and set to work on her hair. It was horribly tangled. What she wouldn't give for a bottle of conditioner right about now.

One of the men had left her a comb made from what appeared to be ivory. Carved with flowers and vines, it was a work of art.

A knock sounded at the door. "Wait just a moment."

Lucy picked up the dress, held it in front of her and called out, "You can come in."

Albin came in, his arms full of some type of clothing. He took one look at her and hastily turned around, his face red as a tube of lipstick.

"My lady, forgive me," he stammered. "I should not be here with you. Your reputation."

The laugh escaped before Lucy could hold it back. "I won't move, so you won't see a thing. Are those clothes in your arms?"

The boy turned, blushed again then took a few steps forward, his eyes on the ground. He held out his arms. "A dress from the village."

Lucy tucked the damp dress under her arms and reached out to take the clothing. "I've got them. You can go now."

The boy turned and fled, calling out over his shoulder, "I'll be outside the door waiting, lady."

As the door shut, she smelled something bad. Lucy sniffed. It was the dress. Foul and smelling strongly of the previous owner, who likely never took a bath in her life. She sniffed again. Body odor and some kind of perfume. A lot of it.

Did this dress belong to a hooker? Holding it out to examine the garment, Lucy frowned. There was some kind of undergarment, a chemise, she guessed. Then a shapeless dress that went over her head, though someone had cut the neckline to show off their assets. Considerable assets, from the way the dress hung. Thank goodness for the yellowish chemise.

She didn't have a bra, hadn't needed one with the wedding gown. This would be the first time since she'd developed breasts that she'd gone without a bra. Thankful she'd only been blessed with a B-cup instead of much larger breasts like her sister Melinda, Lucy shrugged and cinched the belt she'd been provided.

Albin dropped a pair of shoes in his haste to leave. It didn't look like it mattered which foot they went on, so she managed the best she could.

The smell of body odor, perfume and something else she'd rather not dwell on kept making her cough. No way this was going to work.

Lucy pulled the door open to see Albin sitting at a table in the huge kitchen.

"Albin. Thank you for the dress. Er, did it come from a hooker?"

The boy looked at her, a blank expression on his face. "Hooker?"

He seemed young, but they were in medieval England so he should know what she was talking about. "You know, a woman who is given money in exchange for sex."

After a moment, his face brightened.

"My lord gave me coin to buy your clothing. The wench from the inn in the village sold it to me." He scrunched up his face. "I think she's one of the lasses the knights visit when they go into the village. I don't know if they give her coin." He blushed again then looked her up and down.

"She's much, er, well." He made cupping motions over his chest. "Larger than you, lady."

She grinned. "How old are you?"

He made her a bow. "I am eight." Albin stood tall and puffed out his slight chest. "I arrived a few days before Lord Blackford. I was sent to foster with him. He is the most fearsome knight in all the realm. 'Tis most fortunate for me to foster with him." Pride filled his face, making Lucy smile. She'd always wanted a little brother.

"You are very grown up for eight." She plucked the dress away from her body, worried the smell would make her stink again after she felt clean for the first time since arriving here in jolly old England. *Old* being the key word.

"It was very nice of you to find me a gown, but I think I must wash it first."

The boy's face fell. "Have I failed you, my lady?"

She went to him, placing a hand on his shoulder. "Not at all. You see...my nose is most sensitive, so the lovely perfume the lady wore is too strong."

Albin seemed to think about what she said then his face brightened. "You can wash it in the tub, but what will you wear?" He looked scandalized. "You can't go around without any clothes. 'Tisn't proper."

"I have an idea, but I'll require your assistance."

Chapter Eight

Lucy hesitated in the kitchen as her stomach rumbled. "I think I missed lunch."

The man everyone called Cook turned and scowled, but his tone told her he wasn't angry. "Come, girl, and take some food. I have bread, cheese and some nice cherries."

"I love cherries, thank you."

He put the food on a platter, handed it to Albin and then handed her a ceramic jug. "Wine."

She smiled at him. "Thank you, Cook. I don't know your name."

The man looked to be in his late fifties, with sparse gray hair and sparkling blue eyes. He had a limp when he walked.

"Most call me Cook. My name's Bertram, lady."

"Please, call me Lucy." She turned to Albin. "Why don't we have lunch together?"

"Yes, my lady." He grinned at her and darted for the stairs. Lucy gathered up the garments and the wine then turned to Bertram. "Do you know, is there a pot or cauldron of some sort in Will…er, Lord Blackford's room? I want to wash the dress Albin brought me."

"Aye." He was busy making something that resembled stew, but she wasn't sure what kind of meat he was putting into the huge cauldron. Wasn't certain she wanted to know, either.

At the top of the stairs, the door to what she'd begun to call her room stood open. In reality it belonged to William. She knew he was sleeping in the room across the hall from her, and wondered if it was as nice as his.

Albin had cleared the papers and books to one side of the desk. He'd set out the food and stood waiting.

"Thank you. Let me just get the water boiling and we can eat."

The boy darted to the pot and filled it from the pipe. He was stronger than he looked as he carried it over to the fire and set it on the hook to boil. Now she'd seen the pipe, Lucy wondered why she hadn't noticed it before.

"Is there any more soap?" He looked at her in alarm then ran out of the room. It had only been a few minutes when he returned holding a whitish-gray lump in his hands.

"Thank you, Albin. You can put it in the cauldron."

The pot was just big enough to hold the dress and chemise. Lucy turned to him. "Could you turn around while I change clothes?"

The boy looked so embarrassed he ran out of the room, calling out over his shoulder, "I will wait in the hallway until you are dressed." The door shut and Lucy stripped out of the smelly garments.

There was nothing else for her to wear. The tattered wedding dress would have to do. She pulled the dress back on, wincing when it ripped again. This time down the side as she wriggled into it. It had shrunk. Barely resisting the urge to swear, Lucy shimmied and pulled until she managed to get the damp dress on and zipped up.

She looked at herself and started to laugh. Talk about a disaster. She'd make a perfect candidate for one of those reality shows where they make you over.

Opening the door, Lucy peered into the dim hallway. "There you are. You can come in now."

The boy trotted in, took one look at her then made a face before hastily averting his eyes.

"That bad, is it?"

He sniffed. "Not for me to say, my lady."

At his tone, she almost burst out laughing.

"You must be starving. I know I am." She motioned him to a chair. "Let's eat."

The boy came around the table and pulled her chair out. She blinked before sitting down. Somehow in the past few minutes she'd almost forgotten where she was, or rather when. Things were very different now, and she needed to behave as was expected from a lady. There was enough speculation about her as it was. She didn't need anyone saying she had dreadful manners on top of everything else. The two of them sat and ate, both almost inhaling the food.

"So, Albin, how long have you been with Lord Blackford?"

"Been with?" The boy stopped shoveling food in his mouth long enough to look up at her.

"I mean, how long have you served him?"

He wiped his mouth. "I haven't lived here very long, my lady. Lord Blackford was away fighting with the king until he was injured." He took another bite of bread and chewed, talking with his mouth full. "Did you know he's one of the greatest warriors in all the realm?"

Not waiting for a response, he continued brightening to what was obviously a favorite subject.

"He saved the king's life—well, the old king. Now his son is king."

"King Edward II. How was William injured?"

Albin looked at her, a thoughtful look on his face. "You call my lord by his given name."

"I guess things are a little different where I come from. You were telling me?"

"He saved the king's life during battle. A knight killed the king's horse. The animal fell and three other knights came, raising their swords to kill our king." The boy paused to make sure he had her full attention.

"But Lord Blackford drew his blade and ran them through before they could kill the king." He sat back to make sure she was appropriately impressed then continued. Albin was a natural storyteller.

"To show his gratitude, the king awarded my lord Blackford castle. Now he is Lord Blackford. My liege is a most powerful knight." Albin stuffed a piece of cheese in his mouth, washed it down with the watered-down ale and made a face.

"When I arrived to foster with my lord, the castle was much as you see it now. Clement arrived mere days before me. He was supposed to make the castle ready for my lord's return." He wore such a disdainful look on his face that it took Lucy everything she had not to laugh out loud.

Albin leaned over the table and lowered his voice. "I think Clement prefers to eat and visit the village wenches rather than overseeing the needs of Blackford."

"I believe you're right. He is rather plump." Lucy said, hoping he would continue. Wanting to find out more about her mysterious benefactor.

"Did you know there are secret passages here in the castle?"

"Really? I'd love to see them."

The boy looked around as if making sure no one was listening. "I don't want Clement to find out about them. I do not care overmuch for him."

"Your secret is totally safe with me." She'd get him to show her one of the passages later. Maybe she'd find a clue telling her how to get back home? Not like she could sit around and do nothing.

Satisfied, he belched and then grinned, looking like a little boy instead of a very young man. "My lord returned a few weeks after I arrived. Then you appeared. Some of the knights think you're a witch." He gave her a very serious look. "Are you? Could you turn into a bird and fly away?"

She burst out laughing. "I'm not a witch, though I think it would be rather fun to turn into a bird and fly high up in the sky." At that moment, a raven cawed outside, making Albin jump.

"Really, I'm not a witch."

He seemed a bit uncertain, so Lucy gave him her most dazzling smile, hoping to put him at ease.

"If I were a witch, wouldn't I conjure new clothes to wear?"

Albin took a sip of his ale and looked at her curiously. "How did you come to be here, my lady?"

"I would also like to hear the lady's answer." The door opened and the man himself strode in. How long had he been outside the partially open door listening? For the boy wouldn't dine in the chamber with her unless she left the door partway open. He said it wasn't proper.

"The clothing Albin procured was not suitable?" William gestured to the tattered gown she wore as he stood there looking devastatingly handsome. Which told Lucy she needed to stay far, far away from him.

"I greatly appreciate the clothes. It's just, well, the woman it came from...let's say she smelled rather strongly, and I believe she was engaged in one of the oldest professions in the world."

A tiny smile appeared in the corner of William's mouth as Albin worked out what she'd said and made a strangled sound in the back of his throat.

"I see." And that was all William said. A man of few words.

"We were just finishing lunch. Would you care to join us?"

Albin jumped up to pour William a glass of wine. Her host looked sweaty and dirty, and she could smell sweat and horses about him. It wasn't unpleasant, just so different from what she was accustomed to.

William sat down in the other chair with a groan and stretched out his legs.

"I believe, my lady, you were about to tell us where you are from and how you came to be at Blackford."

Lucy had hoped to save this conversation for another time. But by the way they were both looking at her, she had to tell them something. It was always best when lying to stick close to the truth…at least, that was what she'd learned from watching movies and television. America hadn't been discovered yet. Her stomach lurched at the thought.

"The land I come from is far away—North Carolina." She stopped and looked at them to see if William was ready to call for kindling and fire.

"It's in the New World." Both looked perplexed, and she wondered if she were causing all kinds of ripples through history by even saying this much.

"It's very far across the sea. A long ways away. In fact, during the voyage, my ship went down in a storm and the next thing I remember was washing up on the shore alone." So far so good. She took a deep breath and crossed her fingers under the table.

"I made my way up the coast and saw the castle. It was storming and raining, so hard to see. So you see, I don't know how I ended up on the battlements. My head is a bit addled."

William nodded as if her being addled explained a lot. She wanted to smack him and tell the truth to shock him, but then she'd end up as a crispy marshmallow, and she was rather attached to living, thank you very much.

"I want nothing more than to go back home. I don't know if I can." She wouldn't cry. There was nothing she could do for Charlotte and Melinda from here, so she would have to stop thinking about them. Being upset all the time wasn't helping her come up with a plan. Right now, she needed to fit in here until she could find a way back home.

"My escort on the ship must have drowned." Was that the best approach? She wasn't sure, but she went on, "I must go home. My family will think I am dead."

"Your escort was this Simon? The man who killed my knight?" William had a look of speculation on his face. He was smart. She'd have to be very careful around him.

"Simon was my escort."

Liar, liar, pants on fire ran through her head as she talked. "But he must have drowned during the storm, otherwise he'd be here, right? I don't know what happened to your knight. Maybe he was struck by lightning?"

William watched her while Albin sat with his mouth open, hanging on every word.

"You must have been powerfully afraid, my lady." He gulped. "I can't swim."

She reached across the table and patted his arm. "I was very scared."

William stood. "Albin, run along to the stables and see to my horse."

The boy made a hasty bow and scampered from the room.

"Would you join me for dinner in the hall this evening? The food should be edible."

She smiled. "I'd love to."

William got up with a wince, making her wonder if he was still injured. He too made her a bow and left the room. "Until tonight."

Alone, Lucy decided to explore the room a little bit more. She looked through the documents on the desk but couldn't read any of them. Opened a book and couldn't read it either, but she did notice a date on a letter. It was the end of July. So she didn't come through on the exact same day, but a little over a month later. Not to mention the whole "seven hundred years later" bit.

Feeling slightly guilty rummaging through William's things, Lucy bent over the pot simmering on the fire and took a cautious sniff. Not bad. She used a long wooden spoon to lift up the clothes and sniffed again. All she smelled was soap. Happy, she lifted them out dripping. They were too hot to wring out.

With no idea what to do with the soaking wet and heavy clothing, she spread the items over the chairs, pulling them close to the fire to dry. With any luck they'd be dry by dinner.

The trunk at the foot of the bed looked promising. Rummaging through it, she found a tunic-type shirt and what she thought might be leggings.

Like William wore. And my oh my, did he look amazing. The muscles showed, flexing when he walked. Nope, not going there. A pair of boots were next to the desk, but given the size of his feet, no way they'd fit.

Lucy stripped out of the wedding dress, wincing as it ripped again. She held it up. The once beautiful gown was now a stained, tattered mess. Much like her relationship with Simon. As she was standing naked in the room, the door banged open.

"My lady—" William barged in, saw her and stopped, his mouth hanging open.

"Get out! Get out now!" she shrieked. The shredded dress did little to cover the necessary bits.

He hastily backed out of the room. "My apologies, lady. I will be in the hallway."

Chapter Nine

Absolutely mortified William saw her naked, Lucy frantically grabbed at the tunic. She tried on the leggings—were they called hose? They were big on her, but if she belted them they might work. Where was the belt? Right, she'd thrown it in the wash. Opening the chest again, she rummaged around and found a belt. She wrapped it around her waist twice then tied it in a knot in front over the tunic to hold the hose up. From what she could see, she didn't look too bad, if she said so herself.

What to do with the heap of rags that used to be a dress? What if she needed to wear the same clothes she was wearing when she'd landed in William's castle?

It stood to reason she had to wear the exact same outfit she'd arrived in to go back to her own time. She didn't know why she believed it to be true, but she did. Of course, it wasn't as if she'd ever met someone else who'd traveled through time. Lucy snorted to herself. Likely anyone who'd had the misfortune to come to the future found themselves rotting away in an insane asylum.

Deep in her gut, the feeling told her wearing the exact same outfit made sense. Could she trust her faulty gut? With a roll of her eyes, she decided her gut was all she had to guide her, so it would have to do.

Gathering up the dress in her arms, she made a mental note to find some kind of coat to wear over the dress, otherwise someone would be getting an eyeful. Would a coat hinder her from going home? So many questions. Come to think of it, where were the pins from her hair? The shoes?

She rummaged through the room again, shaking out everything she could find. Not a single corner of the trunk escaped her notice. A hollow thump caught her attention. A false bottom. There must be a way to open it. Lucy felt around, and at one corner her finger brushed an indent in the wood. The piece popped loose and there were her blue sparkly shoes and the pins from her hair glittering in the light.

The ruined wedding dress went in next to the shoes before she replaced the false bottom and closed the trunk. At least she knew where everything was when the time came to go home.

Tying her hair back with a scrap of fabric from the dress, she took a deep breath, prayed she wasn't beet red and opened the door. He stood leaning against the wall, arms crossed, one booted foot resting against the stone. When he saw her, he pushed off the wall and made her a bow.

"My apologies, lady. I should not have entered your chambers unannounced."

Heat crept up her neck as he took in her outfit, his left eye twitching. "Is aught amiss with the dress you wore during luncheon?"

She could feel the guilt crawling over her face when she answered. She had the worst poker face ever. "I went through your things looking for something to wear while the clothes Albin found are drying." Lucy put her hands on her hips. "I couldn't very well go around in the dress I arrived in. It has more holes than Swiss cheese. Anyway, as I was saying, the bottom of your truck made a noise."

She pursed her lips. "I knocked on it and it sounded hollow, so I knew it was a false bottom. I opened it and found my shoes, along with the pins from my hair and some of your stuff."

Seeing his look, she hastily added, "I can't read anything in your language anyway. I only speak English." She took another sip of wine. "So I put my dress in with my other things. I have to wear the exact same clothes I arrived in when I go home."

"And why is that, mistress?"

"Superstition, I suppose." It was the best she could come up with without telling him the truth. Lucy went over to check on the clothing. Still a bit damp. She turned them over then looked back at William.

"They're almost dry. When they are, I will change out of your clothes and put the now not smelly dress back on. I hope you don't mind I borrowed them?"

He had an odd look on his face. "You look rather fetching in my tunic and hose." Then William looked embarrassed, as if he'd said too much. "Would you care to join me on a ride? The stables may be in disrepair, but my horses are sound."

"I'd love to. I haven't been on a horse in years."

William looked perplexed. "How do you travel in North Carolina?"

Oops. "We have carriages."

"Of course, my lady." He held out his arm and led her out into the hallway. Several men lounging about in the hall made the sign of the cross as she passed, but Lucy ignored them and continued on to the kitchens.

Bertram turned and looked at her. His mouth made the shape of an O then he dropped the ladle he'd been using to stir some kind of foul-smelling soup on the fire.

"'Tis scandalous, it is, girl. My lord, she cannot dress in such a fashion."

"It's only temporary until my dress dries." She didn't look that bad, did she? Granted, the hose sagged at the knees and the tunic came down to mid-calf, but really, not like she was strutting around in a bikini.

William looked her up and down before turning to Bertram. "I'll have Clement send for a dressmaker." He proceeded to take a loaf of bread, some cheese and wine, which he put into a leather knapsack.

"Come. We ride."

Barely resisting the urge to bark, Lucy followed him outside.

She stopped. And the way she looked up at the horse made William wonder if she'd ever ridden, which was ridiculous. Wasn't it?

"You want me to ride that monster?"

He chuckled. "He has a fine temper, my lady. Shall I assist you?"

William cupped his hands, waiting to help her onto the horse. Lucy Merriweather eyed the animal, looked at his waiting hands in confusion, then seemed to realize the purpose and placed her small foot in his hands. As he tossed her slight form on top of the horse, she let out a muffled "oof" when she landed, making him wince.

"Apologies, my lady."

Wide-eyed, she looked down at him. "I'm okay, just a bit surprised."

Okay? A strange foreign word, no doubt. William stood back and watched as Lucy leaned over the horse to whisper in the beast's ear. And found himself jealous of an animal. Then she looked down at him, his heart stopping at her beauty.

Long brown hair a man could wrap his hands in—he gazed upon her hair and at the horse's tail. She tied her hair up in a fashion to look the same as the horse. The sight should be ridiculous, and yet on her, he found the sight fetching. Gray eyes the color of a winter storm watched him, and for a moment William wanted to lose himself in her gaze.

"What's his name?"

"The horse? Buttercup." He couldn't help the wince that followed, and Lucy started to laugh.

"That's an interesting name for a horse."

He shifted from foot to foot. "I didn't give him the name. The man I purchased him from, his daughter named the beast for the color of his coat."

"He's beautiful." She bent to stroke the animal's ear as the horse gave a soft nicker.

She whispered in his ear, and William found himself leaning forward to hear what she was saying to the beast.

He watched as she closed her eyes, letting out a shaky breath. Her voice came out on a whisper. "Now listen here, Buttercup, you don't throw me off and I won't feed you to the dogs for supper."

William resisted the urge to snort out loud. Instead he pretended to take care of his horse, not giving any indication he had heard her. "Ready?"

She patted the horse and turned to look at him. "Buttercup and I have come to an understanding. I'm ready as I'll ever be."

He swung up into the saddle and they trotted through the

courtyard and under the portcullis. He noticed Lucy looking up at the lethal spikes. At least there was one part of his castle in good repair.

"The rains are coming. Might want to put your hood up, my lady."

William had loaned her one of his cloaks to go riding. And not for the first time, he wondered why she didn't have a cloak. Why she had no escort or other baggage, even if she had washed ashore as she said. Wreckage from the ship should have appeared by now. He would send the men out to search again. There was something strange afoot. And he planned to find out what was going on and who Lucy Merriweather really was, no matter how fetching a wench she may be.

As William rode alongside Lucy, he couldn't help but notice she was uncomfortable in the saddle. Which made him question where had she come from and why she had no familiarity with a horse.

He took pride in showing her his land, even though the fields needed work and he was likely facing a meager winter due to the mismanagement of his lands by his friend and steward.

They came to a spot overlooking the North Sea that was particularly beautiful. It reminded him of her eyes.

"Would you care to rest for a moment, my lady?"

William helped her out of the saddle and led her over to a grassy spot where she could rest. She sat down on the ground with a look of relief on her face.

"I'm not used to riding," she said as she rubbed her backside. 'Twas a fetching backside—not that he noticed overmuch.

Content to watch her stare at the sea, William was startled to notice wetness glistening on her cheek. Nay, not tears. Womanly tears undid him every time. Was she grieving for her home, for a suitor left behind?

"What ails you, my lady?"

She looked up at him, her face so torn with grief it was like a sword to his gut.

"I want to return home."

"No wreckage has been found. By now pieces of the ship should have washed up." He left the rest of his words unsaid and continued, "Is there anyone at all you would have me write to? Let them know you survived?"

"No," she whispered as she stared at the sea. "There's no one at all."

Whilst they rested, the horses munched on grass and William watched Lucy, listening to her talk of the water and the land around them.

She was nothing like Georgina. His wife had had a terrible temper and was as ugly on the inside as she was beautiful on the outside. The rumors plagued him no matter where he went. Grateful to have a home where talk would not reach him, William vowed again never to remarry. Never to trust a woman. For they were full of treachery and lies.

"It's really starting to rain—should we head back?"

She was shivering, dripping wet and looked miserable. William cursed himself for not noticing as he helped her to her feet. As they rode back to Blackford, the thought of having to deal with her and see to the repairs of his home was more than he could bear.

Back inside the walls of Blackford, William helped Lucy down and stepped away quickly. Whenever he touched her it was like being close to the sun. She smelled of summer, making him want to lean closer. Instead he pictured Georgina's face and moved away from his guest.

His recently arrived captain, Wymund, appeared at that moment. "My Lord, look who is newly arrived."

William turned to see a blacksmith known as Osbert walking toward him.

The man made a small bow. "My lord, Edward Thornton sent me to you; thought you might have need of a good blacksmith."

Edward was a fierce warrior and a wealthy distant cousin. One of five brothers. The man obviously still smarted from the last tourney, when William had beaten him soundly and won all the gold. His cousin held a keep in Northern England and was constantly warring with the Scots who raided his cousin's lands.

"You are most welcome, blacksmith." William slapped him on the shoulder, grinning. "We are in need of a stable master and carpenter as well, Osbert. Know you anyone?"

The man thought for a moment. His face brightened and he said, "I have a brother and cousin in need of work. My cousin has a new wife and child to care for. May I send word?"

William nodded. "Tell my steward."

The blacksmith started to speak then shut his mouth.

"What else did my cousin say?"

Osbert turned red. He looked at the ground, kicking dirt around, then took a deep breath and faced William. "He said, 'Tell the whelp William Brandon I should let him rot.' Then he laughed and said he would plan a visit before winter to make sure you weren't starving in your wreck of a castle...my lord."

Lucy gasped. William turned to see her pale and shaking. Did she know Edward?

"My lady, are you unwell?"

"I thought you were Lord Blackford. Your last name is *Brandon*?"

William would have remembered meeting her. His father had died years ago, and he had no siblings. Damnation. She knew. The taint of Georgina followed him home.

He stiffened. "I am William Brandon, Lord Blackford. Get yourself inside before you catch an ague, my lady," he said roughly.

"Wymund. See the lady inside, whilst I tend to the horses."

Just when things were looking up, Lucy had to remind him of
Georgina. If she didn't know him and she didn't know Edward—
was it possible she hadn't simply heard the stories but had known
Georgina? Or was she kin to Georgina's lover? He would watch her,
William thought, as he tended to the beasts. A loose stone fell to the
ground and he cursed. He must see to the repair of his castle before
winter.

Chapter Ten

Brandon? William's last name was the name Simon kept saying was hers. Was he an ancestor? A feeling of dread skittered down Lucy's arm, making the tiny hairs stand up. He had to be the man Simon's ancestor took Blackford from—by force. Simon said the man was a traitor to the crown. What was William going to do this year to get into so much trouble? Why hadn't it clicked earlier?

Clement's last name had to be Grey. One way to find out. She'd find him and ask. She thought again about warning William. What would she say? *Oh, excuse me, you're going to be declared a traitor and your friend Clement is going to take your castle by force. Because obviously you won't give up willingly.*

Who would? Lucy would pour boiling oil down on her attacker's heads, anything to keep such a special place. The castle might be falling down, but there was something magical about it. She snorted. Being thrown back in time was bringing all her childish dreams and fantasies to life.

"My lady? I brought you a cup of warm spiced wine to warm you."

She took the ceramic cup with a smile. "Thank you, Wymund." Wrapped in a blanket, sitting in a chair in front of the fire in the hall, Lucy was finally warm. The rain had chilled her through. Southern girls have thin blood. What if she was stuck here in the past? Where was a crochet hook when she needed one? At least then she could make a sweater for the winter. "Captain?"

The ferocious captain of William's garrison knights turned to look at her. "Yes, lady?"

"Lord Blackford's friend, Clement?" Was it her imagination, or was that a look of distaste on the good captain's face? "Is his last name Grey?"

The knight sat down in the chair across from her, a speculative gleam in his eye. "Aye. Do you know the Grey family?"

Wasn't like she could answer the question without finding herself turned into a crispy marshmallow.

"No, I thought I heard someone mention the name. I've always liked colors for names." Idiot. What a dumb thing to say.

Wymund blinked at her before grinning. "Have many friends named after colors, do ye?"

"Of course. I have friends named Rose, Charlie White, Francis Black and even a Rainbow Runningwolf." Her aunt Mildred, bless her heart, wouldn't be caught dead with a friend named Rainbow.

Rainbow was one of hippie Aunt Pittypat's friends. Like sticking your finger with a needle, a sharp pain pierced Lucy's heart. Aunt Pittypat would be frantic with Lucy presumed dead and Charlotte and Melinda gone. Her eccentric aunt had raised the three of them when their parents were killed in a sailing accident when Lucy was ten.

The knight looked dubious. "What did you hear about the Grey family?"

Maybe he'd give her information. "I heard someone in the courtyard talking. They said William and Clement were friends."

The man refilled their cups and leaned back in his chair. "They grew up together. All of us did. Clement was the third son to the earl. He earned his spurs, though he managed to avoid fighting in any battles. A year ago, the Grey family fell into disfavor with the king and lost everything. William gave Clement a place as steward of Blackford."

The knight looked around the stinky hall and curled his lip. "He was a lazy child and is a lazy man." He met her gaze. "Stay away from him, mistress. The Grey family is a superstitious lot, and he has the notion you are a witch."

He was watching her, waiting. For what? To see if she'd turn into a rat and scurry away?

"Thank you for telling me." She sipped the warm wine. "I'm not a witch. I just want to go home."

"I don't think you are a witch. However, you did appear on the battlements during a storm, and my knight, Alan, is now dead."

She wished she knew how she'd ended up here too. "I didn't kill him. I don't know what happened."

He didn't totally believe her, but let the subject go. When he stood, he looked serious. "I've had a word with the men. They know you are under William's protection, but have a care, mistress."

With those heartening words, he strode out of the hall.

The sounds of tables and benches scraping across the dirty floor woke Lucy with a start. She'd fallen asleep in front of the fire.

"My lady? Lord Blackford requires your attendance at supper." A boy of about fifteen stood before her, waiting.

What was his name? Right. "John. I'm starved. What's for dinner?"

The boy shrugged. "Likely stew and bread." He looked off into the distance. "I miss my mum's cooking."

Good. She wasn't the only one who thought the food tasted awful. What she wouldn't give for a homemade biscuit. Bertram was a better handyman than cook. Why didn't William bring someone in from the village?

Lucy took the boy's arm and sat at a table with William and his knights. She looked around, noticing for the first time there weren't any women around. Not a single one other than her. How odd.

The stew was served in a bread bowl. She couldn't identify the meat and wasn't sure she wanted to. There were veggies cooked down to mush, but overall it wasn't terrible. Ceramic jugs kept the wine and ale cool. There was some type of brown bread, which she eyed with trepidation. Would it crack a tooth?

Lucy took another bite of stew. It didn't taste too bad, and at least it was warm and filling. As long as she didn't think about what was in it, she'd be fine. If she were stuck here, maybe William would hire her to work in the kitchens. She could make a mean soup. And pizza. She could make pizza.

Was it wrong to mess with history? Nope. As far as Lucy was concerned, if she could make it, what would it hurt? Come on, it was pizza.

Across the table, Clement belched and wiped his fingers across his mouth and then on his shirt. He was a disgusting man with food stains on the front of his tunic. He drank his ale, spilling some down the front of him. When he smiled, she could see several blackened and missing teeth.

Note to self, find a way to brush your teeth. She shuddered and turned her attention back to the knight on her left, who was explaining how to knock your opponent off his horse during a joust.

The rest of the knights gathered up and down the long tables seemed to have better manners. They used the tablecloth to wipe their hands and didn't hog all the rolls. The sounds of male voices filled the air, and with the heat from the huge fireplaces, Lucy felt herself growing sleepy.

She tried the brown bread and found it full of rocks and other gritty bits. Ugh. She put it back on the table and eyed her stew bowl. At home she'd always eaten the bread bowl, so she thought why not. The bread was crusty as she ripped off a piece of the bowl and put it in her mouth, chewing. It wasn't too bad, so she took another piece and ate it.

One of Clement's foulmouthed friends shot her an incredulous look, making her feel like she had committed some kind of terrible faux pas.

"Lady, the trenchers go to the poor. We do *not* eat them." He sniffed at her.

Horrified, Lucy snatched her hands away from the table and placed them in her lap. She looked up to see several men looking at her with expressions ranging from humor to disgust.

"I see I have made a mistake. Where I come from, you eat the bowl the stew is served in. I really like bread." She was so embarrassed she wished with everything she had the floor would open up and swallow her where she sat. But at that moment William looked at her and winked. He shrugged, picked up his bowl and took a large bite.

Several men watched him. "What? We will give the trenchers to the poor tomorrow. 'Tis her custom. We should follow suit, no matter how strange it seems, to make the lady feel comfortable. As likely some of our customs seem strange to the lady."

She smiled at him, grateful he'd saved her from feeling like a complete idiot.

Two small boys brought out a tray of what smelled like hot pies. Lucy sniffed—yes, cherry pie. Her stomach rumbled, and saliva pooled in her mouth. Dessert, the best part of a meal. She'd missed it so much. She couldn't wait to try the pie. And there was no Simon to frown and make a comment on the size of her thighs.

Lucy froze. It was the first time she'd thought of her ex without wanting to kill him or weep for what he had done. Grateful for the knowledge she would move forward with her life no matter what happened to her, Lucy accepted a large slice of pie from a serving boy.

How many boys were living in the castle? There seemed to be a never-ending stream of them running to and fro. She wondered, were they sons of the men here? Had they been sent to foster here, like Albin? Or was the most likely explanation that they were orphans William had taken in? She smiled at him, and as she raised her spoon to take a bite of the pie, it slipped off, falling to the floor with a soft plop.

At that moment a rat scurried out from under the muck on the floor, snatched the morsel and ran over to a corner to enjoy his treat. Lucy seemed to be the only one who noticed. The rat greedily consumed the morsel then started to wash his paws and face. The beast was obviously quite pleased with himself. As she smiled, the rat fell over and started to convulse.

The scream left her mouth before she could stop it. "No! Something's wrong with the pie."

Some of the men were looking at her as if she were some kind of hysterical female. Others put their spoons down, looking a bit gray. William jumped up, came around to her and leaned over her shoulder.

"Where, my lady?"

Lucy pointed to the corner where the rat lay, unmoving. William strode over, kneeled down and picked up the rat, looking at the creature. There was still a tiny piece of pie smeared on the rat's face. He leaned close and sniffed, frowning.

He stood up, rat in hand. "Who has eaten the pie?" Several knights stood. "How do you fare?"

The men looked nervous, but none fell to the floor. The rest were watching with looks of horror on their faces.

William held the rat for all to see. "The pie has been poisoned."

Men swore. Lucy heard the unsheathing of blades as they looked about for enemies. She thought she saw a look of satisfaction cross Clement's face, but it was gone so quickly she couldn't be positive.

"There is treachery afoot," William bellowed. "A traitor in our midst."

He met the gaze of every man in the room. Clement met his gaze unflinchingly. William looked speculatively at the man for a moment before turning back to her.

"Are you well?" He pulled the chair out and offered his arm. "Shall I show you to your room?"

"Please. I'm feeling a bit faint."

He turned to the men. "Wymund—"

"I have sent men to search the castle, my lord." The captain of the guard nodded and strode out of the hall.

"Thomas. You will take first watch outside the lady's door tonight."

The young man jumped to his feet, following them up the stairs.

"My lord?" She gulped. "I think Clement tried to poison me."

"Why would someone want to poison you, my lady? I have many enemies—'tis most likely one of them." William narrowed his eyes at her. "A serious charge against my steward. Have you any proof? Clement and I are like brothers. We grew up together." William stomped up the stairs. "He is lazy and arrogant. However, he is a knight. He would not kill a woman."

She shrugged. "He thinks I'm a witch. Seems to be reason enough in this day and age."

He looked at her a question in his eyes but didn't say another word until she was in the room. William paced back and forth in front of the fire before turning to look at her.

"Methinks it is time for you to tell me the truth how you came to be on the battlements at Blackford."

Chapter Eleven

Clement muttered to himself as he paced back and forth in front of the fire in the third-best chamber. By all rights, Blackford should belong to him, not William.

He should be Lord Blackford. 'Twas a stroke of good fortune, William naming him steward. He set about eating his way through the larder, spending the gold William sent and allowing the castle to fall into disrepair. Enough to be worrisome, but not enough he could not undo the damage. For Clement didn't want to have a great expense when the castle belonged to him.

Then the witch showed up. Clement had seen the ravens hanging about the castle. She spoke to them. Sent them to spy on him. He had not determined how she had shown up on the battlements in the middle of a great storm, late at night. Only that it must be witchcraft. How a mere woman managed to kill one of William's knights was a mystery. She must know powerful incantations.

The witch had mistaken him for someone else. A man she was angry with. 'Twas passing strange, as he had no brothers…except one, and they looked nothing alike. That his brother didn't see their father in Clement made his heart ache. For they shared the same father.

He had failed to poison the witch tonight. Lucy Merriweather called upon her unholy skills, called the vermin to her and thwarted his plan to end her. Now William would be on alert, searching for the traitor within the castle.

Clement would fashion new plans. He must not fail. Now that his family had fallen into disfavor with the king, there was no other path open to him.

Nothing else to be done except ensure William was declared traitor to the crown. Then he would show the king the letter his father wrote. His real father. Declaring Clement his son. The letter would be enough for the king to take Blackford, the title and William's gold, and bestow it upon Clement. Who instead of being Clement Brandon had the misfortune to be Clement Grey. William was his half-brother, though the man did not know.

When Clement's mother died, he'd searched her trunks and found the letter. She'd written to William's father, told him she was with child. Named him as the father. William's mother fell ill soon after bearing William and was barren. The earl, wanting many sons, looked elsewhere. Clement knew he was one of possibly many bastards roaming the countryside. William, naïve and believing his father to be a good man, had no idea.

William was under the woman's spell and would not allow her to be burned, as a witch needed to be. Clement would find a way to make her death look like an accident. Then, when the time was right, he would strike out against William, and take back what should be rightfully his.

He remembered the last time he'd seen his real father. Hugh

Brandon was a tall man, with sandy blond hair, smiling brown eyes and a warrior's body. Clement inherited the hair and the eye color, but not the warrior's form. In that he favored his mother and ran to plumpness.

William, on the other hand, had inherited his mother's looks. From the dark hair to the bright green eyes that looked into a man's soul, William was tall and well fashioned. A warrior of renown throughout England and France.

His childhood friend was bewitched by the strange Lucy Merriweather. Clement had watched her, saw her strange doings. Heard her unwholesome songs of incantation when she thought no one was around. He had spent his time at the castle well, knew the secret passages. Would use them to his advantage when the time was right. Clement would have his chance to kill the witch. Once and for all.

William shut the door to the chamber with a bang. Removed from his own bed by a mere girl. The household was in shambles, the floors covered in muck and the walls falling down around his head. The hall reeked with all manner of foul odors. He'd never noticed the stench until she arrived and wrinkled her fetching nose.

He paced in front of the fire. The daft girl was lying to him, he was sure of it. A knock on the door interrupted his grumblings. "Come," he bellowed.

Clement approached. "Is aught amiss, my lord?"

William crossed his arms over his chest and leaned against the wall. "The lady believes you tried to poison her."

"I would do no such thing to Mistress Lucy," Clement sputtered. "She is a witch, my lord. The evil creature would curse me." His friend wrung his hands. "I believe your immortal soul to be in danger. She has bewitched you."

William blew out a sigh. "You have been superstitious since we were children. I tell you again, she is no witch."

Clement looked unconvinced. "Mayhap the pie was meant for someone else, my lord."

"There is treachery afoot. I mean to find out who is behind these doings." Many of the jealous nobles were known to use poison. Let his enemies come. William would dispatch them with a smile. For he missed battle, missed the feel of steel in his hand. Mayhap he was not meant for peace.

"My lord?"

William looked at his steward. "Did you require something else?"

"Let me send for a priest. He will determine if the woman is a witch."

"No. The matter is settled. Tomorrow we shall review the ledgers." Was it his imagination, or did Clement look worried?

"As you wish, my lord." His steward scurried away, no doubt to finish eating through the remains of William's meager larder.

He barred the door, then poured a cup of ale and stared at the trunk. It had been moved to his room along with some of his other things. Her strange clothes were in there. He knelt, opened the lid and rifled through the contents. With a click, the false bottom opened and William removed the odd-looking footwear. Lucy Merriweather could not have walked far in shoes such as the ones he held. They were beautiful yet looked to be fashioned to torture the wearer.

He picked up one of the pins for her hair. It sparkled, catching light from the fire. He had never seen such fine craftsmanship. The gown, reduced to rags, was made of a material so fine, William wondered exactly where she had come from.

Might Clement be correct? Was the piece of pie meant for someone other than Lucy? For him? There were sinister doings happening at Blackford. Some unknown person was causing trouble. But why?

William threw open the shutters, letting the sea breeze into the room. Most likely Lucy ran away from her betrothed. Mayhap the man sent her away, for she could be shrewish.

The thought was enough to make him laugh. She was no shrew —she was pleasant and beautiful. Her gray eyes always filled with sorrow. The haunted look reminded him of men who had survived battle only to become walking corpses.

When was the last time he'd laughed? William couldn't remember. He thought it had been years. Mayhap he had grown out of laughter as some lads grew out of getting spots on their faces. Laughter was merely an affliction, something purged out of the body as one aged.

He wasn't sure how long he paced back and forth in front of the fire thinking about her. The moon was high in the sky when he heard the door to her chamber open. What was she about at this late hour?

He opened the door and followed, keeping to the shadows of the corridor. She made her way onto the battlements. William pressed into the shadows and listened to his guard greet her.

"Off to walk again, lady?" the guard said.

She waved her hand around her head. "Just ignore me. You know how much I like to look at the moon."

William moved closer, straining to hear as she muttered to herself. As he watched, she clicked her heels together.

"Abracadabra." She opened her eyes, sighed and closed them again, a fierce look of concentration upon her face.

"I want to go home." She turned in a circle three times. "When I open my eyes, I will be where I belong."

William hardly dared to breathe as he gazed upon her, spellbound. When she opened her eyes, her entire body slumped inward. She sank down onto the bench then jumped up, leaned over and proceeded to examine the stone.

Had she lost her wits? She closed her eyes tightly and resumed mumbling to herself.

"Oh, hell," she said when she opened her eyes and noticed his guard passing by.

William rarely heard a lady swear. Plenty of wenches, but never a lady. He wasn't sure whether to be shocked or to laugh. Lucy Merriweather promptly closed her eyes again and began singing softly to herself.

He had never heard the song as he caught something about *take me home*. 'Twas an agreeable tune. Riveted to the spot, he could do naught but watch her.

Every so often she would open her eyes, a dejected look on her face. Then she'd take a deep breath and screw them shut again. Her anguish was a bolt to his heart. Unable to bear her pain, he moved forward soundlessly and placed a hand on her arm, startling her.

"Come inside, my lady."

The grief in her eyes almost sent him to his knees. He unfastened his cloak and gently settled it around her shoulders.

"Whatever are you doing, my lady?"

"It won't work. I don't know why, but I can't go back."

"Back? Back where?" Mayhap she was addled.

She seemed to realize he was standing beside her, and pointed behind her. "The bench? Did it ever have a stain on it?" At his blank look she continued, "A mark that looked like blood?"

The hair stood up on the back of his neck as he felt a pain in his breast. Could she see the future? He shook his head to clear it.

"No, my lady. Why do you ask?"

She huffed out a breath. "Just wondering."

William decided it best not to worry overmuch on things he could not change. He did not believe in the fey folk, but she made him wonder. He offered his arm to escort her back to her chamber.

At her door, he patted her on the shoulder, making her stagger. "Bar the door. Things will look better on the morrow."

"Will they?" She favored him with a slight smile. "Thank you. For your company tonight."

Her smile was like a blazing sun. He bowed. "'Twas my pleasure, my lady."

"Lucy. My name's Lucy."

"Good night, Lucy."

"Night, my lord."

He turned and smiled. "You may call me William."

"Okay. Night night, William. Don't let the bed bugs bite."

Shaking his head, he turned on his heel, smiling as he heard the bar slide into place.

Lucy flopped on the bed, listening to the mattress crunch beneath her. She'd failed again. Every night since she'd fallen through time, she went up to the battlements and tried everything she could think of to go back home. The guards were used to her and barely gave her a glance as she went about her strange doings, as they called them.

Her heart broke again as she thought of her sisters. Dead. But then again, they wouldn't be born for hundreds of years. It was a sobering thought. Lucy missed her home, with its creaky old floors, leaky plumbing and nosy neighbors. And my oh my, how she missed Pepsi. And pizza. Let's not forget chocolate. At least they had wine here. Good wine.

What was she missing? In the folktales she'd read as a child, people that vanished usually came back. She racked her brain, thinking of every detail of the night she came through. It was the first day of summer—did that have something to do with it? And the storm. The rain and the lightning.

If she had to wait for the first day of fall, she'd be here for a couple of months. Nonetheless, she'd keep trying, because if she gave up, she'd have to accept she couldn't save her sisters. Then again, who was to say she'd go back on the same date she left? She'd arrived here a month later. Would she go home a month later? Or earlier?

Earlier and she could change things.

She needed a plan. The mattress rustled and Lucy shivered, thinking of the bugs that were surely crawling around inside, and her skin started to itch.

How had her judgment become so skewed? Or was it that you never really knew the person you were with? Had Simon hidden his true self from her?

Trust. A simple word, yet so hard to put into practice. She was afraid. To try again, to open up to another person. No matter how interesting William was, what if she was wrong about him too?

It seemed like Lucy tossed and turned for hours before she gave up and moved to the chair in front of the fire. Over and over she twisted her hair through her fingers, trying to come up with some way that would take her back home. To the future.

As morning light filtered into the room, Lucy stood and looked out at the water. She'd come to a decision. It was time to put on her big-girl panties and face the ugly truth. Trapped in medieval England with no clue how to get back to the twenty-first century, she had to move forward.

Her head ached from all the questions, all the worry. If only she had a packet of Goody's Headache Powder. That bitter-tasting powder signaled relief. And Pepsi. *Stop. All you're doing is drooling on your shirt. Stop thinking of what you cannot have.*

It was time to figure out how she was going to blend in, since it looked like she was stuck here permanently. Maybe William would hire her to work in kitchens? Heaven knows she could come up with something better. The food stank.

As she closed the door in her head to the future, a tiny glimmer of light shone through the keyhole. If another thunderstorm raged, she would go to the battlements and try again. And on the first day of fall, September twenty-third, she would try one last time.

Then she would accept her fate.

Chapter Twelve

Lucy spent the day with William. He introduced her to the inhabitants of his lands. She didn't like the word *peasant*, but *worker* didn't fit either. It wasn't like they could quit.

"Could we visit the village?"

"Aye. I will take you tomorrow, if you like."

Before she could answer, a guard came running toward them. William had a hand on his sword, ready for trouble.

"My lord, come quickly. One of the men found a body." The guard looked at her, and Lucy recognized him from the morning she woke on the battlements.

"The man is dressed in odd garments."

"Where?" William demanded.

"When we searched the cove, we didn't go far enough around the western side. The tide was coming in. The man is wedged into the rocks."

William took off at a jog, making Lucy run to keep up with his longer legs. She didn't know why, but she had the feeling she needed to see the man.

Could it be?

She'd been planning to take the path down to the cove later today and dip her toes into the sea. As they made their way down the path, her apprehension grew.

Two of William's men stood waiting. A third called out, "Up here, my lord."

He turned and looked at her. "Stay here."

"Please, let me come with you." She placed a hand on his arm.

Lips pressed together, he seemed about to refuse and then changed his mind. "Come along, but be careful—the rocks are treacherous."

He scrambled up the rocks as if he were a goat. She picked her way up, stumbling and grasping for a handhold when William reached down, put his hands on her hips and lifted her over a particularly large rock. He set her down on a flat stone. A piece of cloth was wedged in the rock to her left. William bent over and picked it up. The cloth looked to have been blue at some point. The color his men wore.

The guard leaned close to William. "'Tis a piece of Alan's tunic." The man pointed to a large rock a few feet away, where Lucy could see a piece of cloth sticking out. "Over here."

She followed, her sense of unease growing greater with every step. There, wedged into the rock, was the broken body of a man. The breeze shifted and Lucy started to gag.

The body was badly decomposed from the elements. She started to turn away when something caught her eye. Trying to breathe through her mouth, she bent over and let out a gasp.

William's expression darkened. "You know this man?"

The world started to spin. She felt her insides heave, but at least this time she threw up on the rocks instead of his boots.

"Simon. What took y'all so long to find him?" She was shaking so badly, she didn't realize her teeth were chattering until the clicking sound made her bite the inside of her cheek to stop. William put a hand under her arm to steady her.

"The current is treacherous on this side of the cove—mind your step. He has been here quite some time, my lady. The sea air is not kind."

He was nice enough not to mention how birds or other animals had eaten parts of him. Her stomach rolled thinking about it.

One of the guards looked at William. "He fell from the battlements. If he had washed out to sea we never would have found the body, or it would have washed ashore days ago."

William nodded. "I'm sorry for not believing you when you said there was a man with you, lady." He looked at the men. "Give the lady a moment then take the body to be buried in the plot behind the chapel."

The men moved away, giving her space. So many emotions ran through her, Lucy was having a hard time thinking clearly. "I recognize his suit and cufflinks." She pointed at the arm sticking out at an unnatural angle.

William looked at where she was pointing and leaned closer. She heard him inhale sharply.

"The crest carved into the gold—a boar's head. A rose in its mouth." He pointed at Simon's cufflink. "The Grey family crest."

Normally William's skin had an almost golden hue from all the time he spent outdoors, but right now he looked about the color of milk. Lucy worried he might be the one to faint. There was no way she could catch him. The man had to outweigh her by a hundred pounds.

He leaned closer, ignoring the terrible smell, and looked at what remained of Simon's face. "Clement has no other family. But this man is clearly kin to the Grey family. He looks like Clement. They could be brothers."

He probably didn't realize his hand was on the hilt of his sword, and Lucy took a step backward, stumbling before she caught herself.

"I ask you again, my lady. Who is this man?"

A raven called out, circling above them. Lucy took a moment to watch the bird before meeting William's sharp gaze. She took a deep breath, but before she could answer he said, "Such fine craftsmanship. I recognize not the clothing he wears." He watched her closely. "But 'tis similar to the clothes you were wearing when you arrived on my battlements, lady."

He fumbled with the cufflinks, trying to remove them. "No one is to know of this." His hand went to a knife at his belt and she stopped him.

"Please," she said softly, "let me."

You can do this, Lucy Merriweather. Don't think about the body as a person. Simon is long gone. This is nothing more than a shell left behind. It's the same as going to a funeral. You can do this.

She swallowed, moved next to the body and knelt down. This close, the smell was almost overwhelming. If it wasn't for the breeze she thought she would've been sick again.

As fast as she could, she removed the cufflink, handed it to William then looked for the other. The arm seemed to be wedged under the body. No, it wasn't attached to the body. She started to gag and forced herself to swallow. Weakly, she looked up at William and pointed. "Can you move him so I can reach the other one?"

He moved Simon enough for her to remove the cufflink and drop it in his hand. The watch. No one could see it. Lucy took it off his wrist, trying to forget all the times his hand had held hers. She handed it to William, who looked at it curiously then added it to the pouch at his waist.

"Best not to let anyone know about or see these." He looked at her and she nodded.

Her stomach was done waiting. She scrambled down the rocks, slipped a couple times, skinned up her calf and made it all the way to the sand before she barfed.

From somewhere far away, she heard William call out, "Remove the body. I will see the lady to her chamber."

And then there was only blackness.

Lucy opened her eyes to see a raven sitting on a rock watching her. What was it with the big birds? Ever since she'd arrived in England she'd seen them everywhere. From the one at the tiny cottage with Simon to another almost every day or every few days here at the castle. William should have had a raven on his shield instead of a hellhound.

She was leaning against something soft. Her elbow dug in as she sat up.

"Oof."

"Sorry." The soft rock was William.

"Feeling better?"

"I swear, I've never fainted this much in my entire life." She tilted her head, looking up into his face. For a moment they simply looked at each other. The raven cawed, took to the air and broke the spell. He looked away first.

Simon being thrown back in time with her rocked her to the core. Why? For what purpose? Because he'd been outside so long, she couldn't tell exactly what had happened, but the gash running from his neck down through his shoulder seemed to be what killed him. Her insides heaved from thinking about the injury.

Simon was dead.

Cold, hard truth flooded through her veins. She was alive because the guard, Alan, had killed Simon before he could kill her. He didn't deserve her guilt. Nor would she feel sorry for her ex. Another truth rattled around inside her brain. She snorted. She'd gone from being married to being a widow in less than a night. Had to be some kind of record. Even celebrity marriages lasted longer.

Hazy memories surfaced from the night in question. Fragmented images of Simon punching her, hands locked around her neck and the night lit by lightning, with blood raining down. The guard must've stabbed him.

Alan had saved her life. She would be forever grateful. William said he had no family. Lucy thought for a moment. She would plant flowers in his honor. It was a small thing, but at least it was something she could do to mark his sacrifice.

How did you thank someone for saving your life?

Chapter Thirteen

The words William spoke washed over her like water smoothing out the sand. Everything a soft blur. She was up on her feet racing up the path before she'd made the conscious decision to go.

As she ran into the middle of the courtyard, she hunched over, hands on her knees, breathing heavily.

There had to be someone who would know.

"Lucy. What ails you?" He spoke softly to her as he would to a skittish horse.

How could he understand?

"I need a witch. She's the only one who can help me." A tear slid down her face as she wiped it away.

There was a man watching her. She ran up to him. "Do you know where I can find a witch? Is there one in the village?"

He gasped in horror, crossing himself before backing away.

The next two people she asked did the same. One even spat on her shoe.

"Cease," William bellowed. He picked her up, slung her over his shoulder and stomped inside past the gawking observers.

Her tarnished knight in this nightmare of a fairy tale grumbled and swore all the way up the stairs and into the chamber. He kicked the door closed and tossed her on the bed like a sack of potatoes. Well, potatoes were probably treated more gently. At least the jolting ride up the stairs and through the air to land on the mattress snapped her out of what was shaping up to be a major hissy fit.

"Have you lost your wits, lady?" William thundered. By the saints, the woman tested his knightly vows with her feebleminded ravings.

He paced around the room, mood growing fouler with every step.

"The entire village will demand I toss you into my dungeons then burn you at the stake."

She looked at him, her eyes beginning to leak. Nay, this would not do. Womanly tears undid him.

"I didn't know you had a dungeon." Lucy Merriweather started to blubber. "Are you going to k…k…kill me?" She pointed to his hand, which happened to be twitching next to his sword.

"Blackford doesn't have a dungeon." He stiffened. He did not abuse women. William patted the sword then frowned severely at the wench. She'd been nothing but trouble. Vexing him, taking him away from his duties and causing an uproar among his knights.

"Nay. I will not kill you. Though I am sore tempted." Another tear slipped down her lovely face, making him feel completely helpless.

"Tell me why you risk burning to seek a witch," he demanded. Trying but not wholly succeeding in not bellowing at her.

She looked up at him. "Tell me again. What year is it?"

"Damnable chivalry." With a strained smile he replied, "The Year of Our Lord 1307."

Lucy started babbling so fast he couldn't understand her odd manner of speech. William held up a hand. "I beseech you, stop." He shifted from foot to foot. "Breathe, my lady. Then begin again."

She smiled. A small smile, but it was enough to knock him senseless. What would it be like to have her gaze upon his visage every day for the rest of his life? William made a strangled sound in the back of his throat and gestured for her to continue.

She blew out a breath. Then another. "The morning you and your men found me on the battlements…"

He reached out and thumped her on the back, almost sending Lucy to her knees. "I give you my vow, I will render whatever aid you require. Do not fear me."

"You see. The night before, Simon drugged me…you know, like poisoning? He tricked me into marrying him."

William felt as if he'd taken a blow to the head. Did she love the man they had discovered broken on the rocks? What kind of husband poisoned his betrothed?

"He said there was a curse on Blackford Castle…your castle. It was late, there was a terrible storm and when he tried to kill me… something happened. One minute I was about to go over the wall, the next I woke up here. In the past."

She looked at him for a long moment. "Simon brought me to the castle. His castle. In the year 2015. More than seven hundred years from now."

William wanted to wring his hands as if he were a blubbering woman. He stiffened his back and resisted. She was daft.

He vowed not to shout at her. One did not shout at the witless.

"Have you kin waiting for you?"

Lucy swallowed several times, blinking rapidly. "I have…had two sisters. Simon told me he had them murdered. Now I am trapped here. In the past. I have no hope of ever seeing them again."

"I know a terrible ailment befell you. Mayhap your wits are muddled."

She scowled at him, placed her hands on her hips and poked him in the chest.

"Listen here, buster. The king you serve now? Edward II? He's going to be off the throne in 1327 and then he dies. A terrible death, though now there's speculation as to what really happened. Anyway, in my time, there's a woman on the throne. Queen Elizabeth II."

He scoffed. Poor girl. Beautiful and filled with nonsensical ravings. "A woman on the throne of England? Nay."

Lucy stamped on his foot. "I wish I'd paid more attention in history class. You're laughing about a queen? How about this? We don't ride horses anymore. We have cars. They go incredibly fast and don't need to be fed. We have contraptions allowing us to fly through the air to other countries in a matter of hours. Hell, in my time we've sent men to the moon and back."

She stomped around the room, anger making her even more fetching. This time, he did not laugh.

"Don't even get me started on television, internet, phones. Wait —"

Her face took on a rapturous glow.

"Cheesecake. Chocolate. Pizza. Sushi. Hot showers. Movies and more books than I could ever read in a lifetime." She sat down on the bed, slumped over.

"Icy cold Pepsi."

"Enough." He came to kneel before her, not knowing what to say or how to render aid. He said the first thought that came into his head. "I have books you may read."

With that, he watched in horror as her eyes began to leak. Blubbering ensued.

Not knowing what to do, he sat beside her, gathered her to his chest and thumped her on the back.

"Er…your tale…" He trailed off, not knowing what to say. One thing he knew for sure? She was not from the future. It was not possible, therefore she must be feebleminded. Mayhap from her injuries the morning he found her.

The only sounds were her muffled sobs as William stroked her hair. Her stomach grumbled. She wiped her nose on his sleeve then tilted her head back to look at him.

The anguish in her gaze undid him. William leaned closer, feeling her breath on his face.

A knock sounded at the door. He jerked back. Bloody hell, he'd almost kissed her.

Lucy pressed fingertips to her lips. He'd almost kissed her. One moment she'd been crying all down the front of his tunic, the next his mouth was an inch from hers. Up close, she noticed flecks of gold in his piercing green eyes.

She knelt in a corner of the garden, surveying her work. One tiny spot was now weed free and ready for planting.

"Mistress, will these do?" Albin held up clumps of dirt attached to green leaves and flowers. "I dug up the roots so you could plant them. Five different types. Is it enough?" He knelt down beside her, eager to show off his gift.

"Thank you, they're perfect. Why don't we plant half here and take the rest to plant around Alan's grave?" She smiled at him. "Would he like that?"

The boy frowned, a serious look of concentration on his face. He nodded to himself and gathered up half the flowers. "Alan didn't like womanly things, though I believe he would be happy we are remembering him." He started running toward the little cemetery behind the chapel. "Come on, mistress Lucy."

She laughed. At least he wasn't calling her "my lady" all the time. Thomas stood guard a few feet away, trying very hard to look ferocious. All the boys worshipped William, and she'd caught a few of them practicing his walk and expressions on more than one occasion.

Albin went to fetch a bucket of water from the well to water the newly planted flowers. They'd planted primrose, bluebells, poppies, snowdrops and cowslip that smelled like apricots.

A tear dripped down onto the stone marking Alan's grave. Pretty soon, she was crying so hard she couldn't see. She cried for being so naive, over the loss of her sisters and over a man losing his life protecting her.

Albin was only eight. She muttered a bad word. The kid acted more mature than she did.

With a shake of her head, Lucy stood up, dusting her hands across her skirts.

"Crying doesn't help." She wiped her eyes on her sleeve, stretched and decided to make the best of the situation. Time to grow up.

Chapter Fourteen

After a dreadful breakfast of burned porridge, Lucy was ready to scream. Would it offend Bertram if she asked William if she could help in the kitchen?

She was willing to bet he'd be all about edible food. Since arriving at Blackford, she'd been so wrapped up in accepting she was truly in the past that she hadn't really done much exploring.

After her major meltdown in front of William and the castle inhabitants yesterday, she wanted nothing more than to be left alone to work in the garden or hide in the kitchen and cook.

Simon was truly dead. The part of her who'd fallen for him mourned his loss. But…the small animal part of her rejoiced. She might be trapped in 1307, but at least she knew without a doubt he wasn't in their present. At least Simon would never hurt another soul. If only she knew the fate of her sisters.

Did his death mean history would change? Since he'd died here in the past, how would she meet him in her future? Her head hurt trying to figure out how time travel worked. Finally, Lucy decided time wasn't linear. It had to be made up of many threads. Maybe there was another version of her living her life? Or a version where she died and her thread ended instead of falling through time.

Would scientists one day learn the secrets of time travel? Perhaps future generations would book a ticket much like we do today to fly to an exotic destination, except they would choose the when and where in the past. Or even the future. Lucy snorted thinking about how people might want to tinker with or change history. Talk about a hot mess. Enough trying to figure out how time travel worked.

The sun was shining, and she decided to walk outside the walls and then work her way back to the castle. The portcullis had lethal-looking spikes, and she cringed thinking what it would feel like if they came down on her head. Good heavens, the tunnel itself must be fifteen or twenty feet long. From looking at the walls, she could tell they were thick.

It would be the perfect place to ride out a zombie apocalypse. Talk about being a little paranoid. What kind of enemies were they worried about around here? The map she'd had during the drive to Blackford showed the Scottish border being a little over two hundred and fifty miles away. Did he have enemies closer to home?

The masons were hard at work on the garrison. They mostly kept to themselves, but smiled as she passed by. Looked like they were almost finished. The knights would be happy to have it complete. The salty sea air tickled her nose as she inhaled. Where was the path down to the beach?

She'd love to dip her toes in the water. As she walked around the bailey, she could see what she would only describe as hovels near the far wall to her right. They weren't much better than some of the homeless shanties she'd seen in the city.

For a medieval courtyard, it was a bit lacking, from what her imagination supplied. She expected more activity, more people coming and going. And buildings in better condition. Not for the first time, she wondered why she hadn't paid more attention during history class.

She came to the garden. There were still an awful lot of weeds surrounded by a half-falling-down fence. That was one thing she could do to be useful: she would work in the garden. Over the years she'd learned the hard way that it was always better to have a backup plan. What better way than to make herself useful to the lord of the castle?

The masons said the stables would be finished next. Though from looking at them, she suspected the horses lived in nicer accommodations than the people in the shacks. What did that say about William? Did he care more about his horses than his people? Was he like Simon in that respect? So far she had only seen him treat the serving boys with kindness, but she worried when she wasn't around he was mean to them like Simon.

The grassy field in front of her held an assortment of men. The ring of steel filled the air as she watched the men fight. Some fought with swords, and a couple were shooting arrows. She snickered. Every time one of them let loose an arrow, she wanted to step closer, to see if any of them looked like her favorite crossbow-wielding hottie on *The Walking Dead*.

William stumbled over a rock, swearing fluently as his opponent's sword flashed down next to his ear. A bit closer and he would be looking at his ear on the ground. He'd slept fitfully, visions of a certain beautiful but perplexing wench filling his thoughts. The story she concocted—he knew she believed in what she told him. He believed her not. People could not fly like the birds in the sky. He scoffed. They most certainly would never walk on the moon. Why would she tell him such stories? Stories that would mean her death by burning?

Was it possible she came to him from the future? Her garments were fashioned out of materials new to him. The dress made a ripping sound when he pulled a piece of metal, and then it opened in two. He'd only jumped because he wasn't expecting such a sound, not because it startled him as if he were a small child.

He'd worked up a sweat in the lists all morning and now stood still, looking around for the next person upon whom he might vent his ill humor.

There she was. Lucy Merriweather wore the ill-fitting dress Albin had procured for her from the village. It was too short, and fit tightly around the bosom, showing off her…well, parts of her he didn't want other men drooling over.

"Good morrow to you, lady."

Lucy smiled, and it was as if the sun came out and warmed his skin. "Do you do this every morning?" She waved a hand around the general vicinity of the lists.

One of the knights looked at her like she was addled before crossing himself and scurrying away.

"What's his problem?"

William chuckled. "He is unused to seeing a woman at Blackford."

She gazed up at him, a question in her eyes. Then she turned and looked around, taking in the inhabitants.

"Why aren't there any women here?" She narrowed her eyes. "You're not some kind of Templar knights who think women are evil, are you?"

"We are not Templars." Not bloody likely he would tell her his reasoning for not allowing women. Instead, he said, "Women are a distraction. The men need to train. Prepare to face any enemy. I am no monk. The men may visit the village to tend to their needs. But I will have no women here."

Then he saw her face and chuckled. "It appears I have made an exception, my lady."

"It's Lucy, remember?"

He made her a small bow. "As you wish, Lucy."

William decided to show her what swordplay was all about. Not that he was showing off; rather he would demonstrate his skill so she could appreciate a fine bit of swordplay.

"Would you care to watch?"

"Oh yes, I've never seen a real sword fight before."

He paused. Had she been so secluded that she had never seen men fight with swords? Her story of the future came back to him. Talking to Lucy filled him with more questions than answers.

William offered her his arm, leading her over to a bench against the wall. Seeing her settled, he nodded to Albin. "Watch over the lady."

Albin stood straight and tall. "Aye, my lord. I'll watch over and protect her."

He unsheathed his sword and plunged into the fray, taking on two men at once.

Lucy leaned against the cool wall and pulled the cloak around her. He was a sight to behold. The man fought with grace and a ruthlessness that made her glad she wasn't on his bad side. The blade was an extension of his arm.

Sheesh, he must live, breathe and sleep with his sword. Hmmm, I wouldn't mind being his sword for a night, curled up to him to sleep, although I don't think there'd be much actual sleeping going on.

Stop it this instant, Lucy Merriweather! You have terrible judgment when it comes to men. You are now a widow. Doesn't matter if you were tricked into marriage. I would suggest you better seek some serious counseling before you even consider dating again.

She frowned. Her conscience was right. Might as well enjoy the show.

Clement sat down next to her and didn't even cross himself. Perhaps they were making progress. "Lady, how fare you?" He looked so much like Simon. No, Simon looked like Clement.

"Enjoying this lovely day," she forced out.

"You do not mourn for your dead companion?"

He wore a sly smile on his face. It took everything she had not to smack him.

She decided to ignore the question. He only wanted to get a rise out of her. She pasted on her brightest fake smile. "Don't you train with the men?" *Wimpy loser.*

He curled his lip. "I am in charge of the castle. I do not have time to play with swords."

Sheesh, talk about touchy. He didn't have any of Simon's charm. This guy was Mr. Nasty.

He leaned in close, eyes blazing. "How did you come to be on the battlements? In truth, are you a witch? Was the man your sacrifice to the devil?" He shot her a calculating look. "There is a great deal of coin to be made from powerful potions."

"Sorry, I'm no witch." He was rude and totally crazy.

Clement grasped her arm. "How do you know my sire? I would have remembered meeting a wench such as yourself."

"I was mistaken. You look a lot like someone I know."

"You called me Simon before you struck me. My sire is Simon Grey. The dead man you also called Simon." Clement looked thoughtful. "With most of his face eaten away, 'twas hard to tell what he looked like."

"You're horrible." A warning flashed through her, making Lucy scoot to the edge of the bench. She looked around, seeking out William, and was surprised to see him watching her while he fought. Feeling better, she pulled her arm away.

"Simon is a common name. Nothing more than a coincidence." There was something in his eyes that made her think she was speaking to Simon. The urge to flee was so strong she was standing before she realized it. The earth needed to stop spinning and go back to normal. Cars, people, phones ringing, power lines. Sweet tea and her sisters. Not this whole medieval thing. It was as if she were watching herself onscreen. Talk about surreal.

Out of the corner of her eye, Lucy watched as William re-sheathed his sword, strode over to her and cocked a brow.

"Were you impressed, my lady?"

Grateful for his presence, she handed him a bottle of ale. He accepted the drink with a smile then dragged a sleeve across his face.

"I am most impressed by your skill, my lord."

He looked at her as if he wasn't sure if she were joking or not. Lucy kept her face blank.

Clement sniffed. "When do you depart?"

What? He couldn't leave her here alone with Clement. Something about the man made her skin crawl. The panic she felt must have shown on her face.

"Are you unwell, Lucy?" William took her hand in his.

She shook her head. "I didn't know you were leaving."

"There is a matter requiring my attention. I will not be gone longer than a se'nnight." He tucked a lock of hair that had come loose from her braid behind her ear.

"Take it." He reached into the pouch at his waist and handed her a bag. It was heavy and clinked in her palm. "Gold."

She looked at him blankly.

William smiled. "Pay the seamstress for new gowns and anything else you require."

Clement sputtered. "I will take care of the gold, my lady."

She started to hand him the bag when William stopped her with a hand on her arm. "The lady may see to her own needs."

Nice. She thought Clement was warming up to her, then this. He looked at her like she was the slop trough and he was a big, hungry pig.

William's hand lingered on hers. "Albin will not leave your side." He ruffled the boy's hair. "He's young but good with a blade. I will leave Thomas behind to guard you as well, worry not."

Easier said than done, she thought.

"Hurry, my lady," Albin implored her as he scampered up the stairs and out onto the battlements. Lucy followed him, smiling at his enthusiasm while Thomas trailed behind her, looking very serious about his guard duties.

The guard on duty nodded to them as they lined up to wave goodbye to William and his men. The door opened again. Lucy turned and barely kept from cringing. It was Clement the pig, as she'd begun to call him.

Thomas moved closer to her so Clement was forced to stand

next to Albin.

"Look, lady, there he is." The excitement on Albin's face was contagious.

William turned to look up at them and waved. Albin waved back frantically while Thomas stood looking serious and Lucy smiled and waved, hoping he'd return quickly. She dreaded being left alone with Clement, who would be in charge with William gone. Why couldn't the man see his friend was a jerk?

The odious man in question leaned close to her ear. "I will be watching you, witch. You will not ensnare another man for your foul deeds." His stinky breath made her take shallow breaths through her mouth as he spoke again. "What does a girl know of spending gold? Give me the coin. I will pay the seamstress and provide whatever womanly frippery you may require."

She turned her most severe look on him, the one she used on her sisters when she was annoyed. "William left me the gold. I will manage it myself." She smiled at him sweetly. "But I thank you for your kind concern. Run along now before I ensnare you too."

Clement's eyes filled with horror. The pig crossed himself, practically running away from her. She didn't laugh. Though she wanted to, very much.

With a final look at William's departing back, Lucy patted Albin on the shoulder. "Let's go find some supper. We have a busy day tomorrow."

The boy grinned at her, scampering ahead while Thomas trailed behind them. She was happy to have him at her back. A feeling of dread swept over her, and Lucy hoped Clement would ignore her for the next week. She'd made an enemy of him. The man was up to something devious. But what?

Chapter Fifteen

The next morning as Lucy pulled the ill-fitting gown over her head, a knock sounded at the door.

Albin popped his head in. "Are you ready, my lady? The seamstress is here." He wriggled with excitement, reminding her of an overgrown puppy.

"Coming." She wished for a mirror then decided it was better not to know. Who knew how dreadful her hair looked without modern-day shampoo and conditioner? Likely a terrible case of bedhead. She braided her hair, tying the end with a scrap of fabric, and followed her constant companion down the stairs.

Thomas pushed off from the wall where he'd been standing watch. "Good morrow, lady."

They stopped in the kitchens, where Thomas sat down to break his fast. Albin grabbed a loaf of bread still hot from the ovens.

"A bowl of porridge, my lady?" Bertram held a wooden bowl in his hand.

Lucy wrinkled her nose. "No thank you." She spied cherries in a ceramic bowl and put a handful on a platter along with cheese and bread. The cook handed her a mug of chilled wine.

She'd never drunk so much wine in all her life. The water from the well was cool and refreshing, though it wasn't served with meals. She made a mental note to have Albin fill a pitcher for her later. Let them think her weird; it was the least of her worries.

"Thank you, Bertram."

The cook beamed.

Lucy turned. "Before I forget, could we talk later?" She paused, thinking how to say it without offending him. "You have a firm hand with the men. They listen to you. Might you be willing to tell them to clean the castle?"

He started to bristle, so she stopped him with a smile and kept talking. "I know how cooking for everyone takes up all your time, but if you could deal with the men, I would be happy to cook for everyone while the castle is being cleaned."

"My lord said nothing to me."

"It's a surprise. One of the boys slipped on the floor last night and chipped a tooth. I'd hate for the state of the castle to reflect badly on our lord, wouldn't you?"

Bertram thought then straightened up, pointing a wooden spoon at her. "Can you cook?"

She gave him what she hoped was a reassuring smile. "I can. You would be doing me a kindness to help me not feel useless." There. Appeal to his vanity.

"The hall needs a good cleaning." He nodded. "The boys here can help you. You must be up early to have the morning meal prepared."

"I will. Thank you. You know the men wouldn't listen to a mere woman asking them to clean."

"You can start in the morn." Bertram scratched his nose. And smartly refrained from saying anything about her sex, though he looked like he wanted to with the grin on his face.

Lucy hugged him and followed Albin down the corridor. He led her to a room she hadn't seen yet. It was very masculine inside, with a huge desk, some books on a shelf and a large window overlooking the ruined garden. A fire blazed in the hearth. Even though it was warm outside, it was always chilly inside the castle.

There was a beautiful oriental rug on the stone floor and a tapestry with his crest of the dog…hellhound on it. This must be William's solar. Clement had claimed it for his own while William was away fighting. Looked like the lord had retaken the room.

She rolled her eyes. Poor Clement the pig. Not. *Guess you shouldn't have spent so much money drinking, eating and whoring.* It was interesting how he and Simon looked so much alike. She could see some of the same personality traits, but by the time Simon was born, the gene pool had made him much more refined. A snort escaped. Then again, he had tried to kill her. The polish of manners and civilization simply hid his true nature. Did William hide a bad side too?

Three women stood by the desk. A plump, middle-aged woman, who smiled and immediately reminded Lucy of her next-door neighbor who was always out working in the yard. A pang of longing swept over her. Instead of giving in to sorrow, she shook her head and focused on the fabrics laid out in an orderly line. Two girls around fourteen or so looked her over with faces full of curiosity.

"Good morrow to you, my lady," the seamstress said. "Come see if any of the fabrics please you."

The fabrics were lovely. Everything from wool and linen to silk and velvet. Lucy fingered the velvet and silk, but with a sigh decided she needed to be practical. Linen and wool.

"Two dresses should be plenty."

The woman looked her up and down. "Lord Blackford said you are to have a wardrobe befitting a lady, my lady."

"Please, call me Lucy."

The seamstress smiled. "Mistress. You can call me Jeanne." She clapped her hands and the girls jumped. She turned her eye on Albin. "Off with ye."

He looked at Lucy, who nodded, then scampered out the door, calling over his shoulder, "I will stand guard while Thomas breaks his fast, my lady."

He called her "my lady" whenever people were around. He was starting to relax and call her "mistress" when they were alone. She found herself looking forward to seeing the little imp.

The two girls stripped her down to her birthday suit and measured her. Fabrics were draped across her skin as Jeanne pursed her lips. Sometimes frowning, sometimes smiling. Lucy trusted her to know what to do.

The girls wore what looked like an apron over their dresses. With pockets it would be perfect for working in the kitchen and the garden. Pockets didn't seem to be invented yet. They were so useful. Would she mess up history? Lucy pondered the thought then decided her need for carrying stuff around outweighed whatever historical ripples she might cause.

Anyway, she'd probably already changed history by coming back. And by Simon coming back and dying here in the past.

What could pockets hurt?

"I was wondering, might I have aprons to wear over my dresses?" The seamstress, Jeanne, looked at her as if she had two heads.

"Mistress? A lady does not wear such a garment."

She smiled at the kindly woman. "Well, I plan to work in the kitchen. Have you tasted the food?" She made a face. "And I'm going to plant a garden. I don't want to get my dress dirty. So I'd really like a couple of aprons."

Thomas came in bearing ale for Jeanne and her girls and wine for Lucy. He also brought lunch. Platters filled with chicken and other meats. And bowls of pottage. A rich, creamy soup with Swiss chard and beans mixed in. It had a savory flavor.

Seeing the chicken, Lucy decided she'd make fried chicken Southern style when William returned.

Messing with history seemed to be a slippery slope. What was next?

Another platter contained cheese, fruit and bread. Her favorites.

"Thank you, Thomas." He smiled and left the room. They all dug in. Getting fitted for a new wardrobe was more tiring than she thought.

Finished eating, Lucy held up a piece of fabric in front of one of the girls' aprons. "I'd like pockets on my aprons." She demonstrated with the fabric how it would look. Then she made a pocket and showed Jeanne what she wanted for her dresses and cloak.

The woman looked thoughtful. "I can make this. A new fashion from France?"

Lucy crossed fingers behind her back, hoping she wouldn't be struck dead. "Yes, it is."

"Three pairs of stockings, three chemises, three dresses, a cloak, one gown for courtly doings and..." Jeanne looked at her feet. "Footwear. You need shoes. There is a traveling merchant in the village. Shall I send for him?"

Overwhelmed, Lucy nodded. The fancy dress would be made out of blue velvet and trimmed with white fur. It was simpler than the seamstress suggested, but no way was she having expensive jewels on a dress. William must be very rich. Yet he lived and dressed simply. She hadn't seen any fancy dishes or goblets or clothing. Was it because he'd only recently moved in, or was he one of those low-key guys? She liked he didn't show off his money or talk about it all the time.

She handed the bag to Jeanne. "Is this enough?"

The woman's eyes went round as she felt the bag, and rounder when she looked inside. She fished out a few coins and handed back the bag. "This will do, mistress."

Jeanne spoke to one of the girls then turned back around to Lucy. "Tomorrow is market day in the village."

"Oh. Don't send for the merchant. I'd love to go into the village tomorrow."

The seamstress talked about the merchants and market day. It sounded like so much fun. Lucy couldn't wait. She was busy thinking about something small she could buy for William when the woman's words penetrated her brain. "I'm sorry, what did you say?"

"There will be a gypsy selling love potions and such things. Stay well away from her, mistress."

The two girls blushed, and Lucy wondered if they bought love potions from the gypsy.

Maybe the woman could help her get home. In the stories she'd read as a child, they always had mysterious powers...

Chapter Sixteen

A large, grassy field had been transformed into some kind of medieval market looking like it came straight out of a movie.

People were dressed in their Sunday best. After church they all made their way to the market, laughing and talking. Lucy sniffed. So many yummy cooking smells filled the air. Various vendors set up among the carts and wagons hawking their wares.

She could hear minstrels playing in the distance. Music. For the first time since she'd landed here. What she wouldn't give for her playlist of songs right about now.

Thomas and Albin insisted on escorting her.

"How often does the market occur?" After being at the castle for several weeks, looking at the same people and scenery, the scene playing out in front of her was a feast for the eyes.

"Once a month on Sunday, my lady," Thomas told her as he watched the crowd, one hand on his sword and a scowl on his face. He took his duty very seriously.

Albin was drooling over a vendor selling pastries. Lucy looked at the fruit glistening on the crust and felt her stomach rumble. She bought one for each of them. At one stall she bought a few ribbons for her hair. The piece of fabric she'd been using had finally fallen apart. She ordered two pairs of shoes, feeling slightly guilty spending William's money on something she hoped she'd no longer need soon.

The other evening, at the time between sunset and dark, she had felt something in the air. Hopeful, she climbed the steps to the battlements, placed her hand on the unmarked stone where she thought she remembered the stain and closed her eyes, wishing to go home. In the pouch at her waist she carried her jewelry and pins from her hair. She wasn't wearing the sparkly blue wedges or tattered dress, but she thought maybe the jewelry would be enough.

Nothing happened. Instead of making a fuss, she simply went to bed and, for the first time, didn't cry.

They came to a large space with furniture and tapestries. "Thomas. Albin. Help me pick a tapestry for William…er, Lord Blackford. And some chairs for the hall and chambers."

They looked dubious but gamely walked amongst the offerings. The merchant, sensing a large sale, came beaming out, a mug of ale in his hand.

"My lady. Such a fine day."

Thomas found a tapestry depicting a hunting scene. Lucy thought it would look nice in William's room. The merchant told her the price and she almost gasped. It was like buying a fancy rug. The chairs weren't quite as bad.

"Can you make cushions for the chairs?"

He nodded eagerly. "Whatever the lady of Blackford Castle requires."

"Oh, I'm not the lady of the castle. I'm…" What was she? "I'm a guest of Lord Blackford."

The man smiled. They arranged to have the pieces delivered. She paid and, with her purse much lighter, they went on their way.

"We'll put three of the chairs in front of the big hearth in the hall. One in my chamber and one in William's chamber." She looked at her escorts. "Do you think he'll like it?"

Albin made a face. "Should have purchased a sword or knife."

"He will be most pleased, my lady," Thomas said.

She bought a few costly spices and other things to cook her first few meals. And six laying hens to add to the ones already at the castle. She wanted to make quiche and omelets, so she needed more eggs.

Thomas and Albin were busy looking at a trained bear doing tricks. As Lucy moved toward the most colorful stall, someone pushed her. She tripped over a pile of wood and went down hard, crying out.

"My lady, what happened?"

"Ouch. Damn it, that hurt." She put a hand to her throbbing cheek and eye. A metallic taste filled her mouth. Touching a finger to her lip, she realized her lip was split.

"Someone pushed me."

"Stay with the lady." Thomas moved quickly through the gathered crowd, looking for the person who pushed her.

It felt deliberate. Albin and a couple of people helped her up. A mug of ale was pressed into one hand, a relatively clean cloth in the other.

"Who pushed the lady?" one man called out.

Another spoke up: "I saw a large man with a hood."

No one else seemed to know anything about her attacker.

Lucy winced. She was going to have a heck of a shiner in the morning. Thanking a woman for the ale, she dusted herself off and walked over to the colorful display.

Yarn.

So much to choose from. Lust filled her thinking of all the things she could crochet. She stopped. Crochet didn't exist yet. Not until the early eighteen hundreds. For a few minutes she waffled then shrugged. She'd already made omelets and French toast for breakfast and introduced pockets. What could crochet hurt?

Feeling justified, she bought a bagful of yarn. They had sheep at the castle. She needed to find someone who could spin the wool. Then she could dye it using plants or something. At least she could try.

If nothing else, she would make William and her escorts scarves to keep warm this winter as a thank-you for looking out for her.

"Albin? Is there someone who could carve something out of wood for me here?"

"What, a bowl or some such thing, mistress?"

"Something like that."

He scratched his head. "Osbert's brother has come to stay. He can make whatever you need."

Osbert was the blacksmith. Lucy remembered meeting a man who looked like he could be a brother to the burly redheaded man.

"Perfect. It's getting late and I need to check on my stew for dinner. Shall we go?"

"Will dinner be as good as the meal this morn, my lady?" Thomas looked so hopeful that Lucy smiled.

"Just wait until you taste the meal I have planned when Lord Blackford returns." She tried not to call him William to the men. It felt too familiar. Too intimate. Had he thought about her at all while he was away doing heaven knows what?

Not that she was thinking about him while he was gone. *Yeah, right. And I've got a bridge to sell you,* she thought.

"Albin, would you take the packages to my chamber?" She tried to treat him like a grownup. In her time, he'd be nothing more than a little boy. But here he was expected to live away from his parents.

To learn to fight and serve his lord. A great deal of responsibility for a boy of eight.

"You can have another pastry, but don't spoil your dinner."

He grinned and scampered inside. She turned to Thomas. "Could you help me find Osbert's brother? His name's Norbert, right?"

He nodded, leading her toward the newly repaired hut next to where the blacksmith worked. She could see another shop or work area in progress. Looked like she could have asked him to make the chairs. Once he settled in, maybe he could make her a chaise to have by the fire in her room. It would be the perfect spot to crochet and stare out the window.

The evening light tinged the courtyard in gold. Even the rickety sheds holding the animals looked pretty.

"Thomas. Give me a moment." As she made her way over to one of the adorable black cows with a band of white in the middle, she reached in the pouch around her waist. She'd nicknamed the smallest cow Penelope.

Penelope mooed. "Jeez, have some patience." Lucy brushed the slightly wilted lettuce off on her dress. "Don't tell Bertram. He doesn't think you need treats." Lucy offered the handful of greens to Penelope, laughing as the tongue swiped across her palm.

"Yuck. Where's hand sanitizer when I need it?"

She leaned back against the fence, stretched out the kinks in her back and, for a moment, simply enjoyed her surroundings.

Life here was hard, yet simpler in many ways. There was a rhythm to daily life in the castle. From the meals to the peasants coming and going to the knights fighting in the lists. Lucy thought she could enjoy this life. Here in this time.

"Mistress."

Lucy jumped. The man in question was stocky like his brother, with the same curly red hair and ruddy complexion.

"Did I startle you, my lady?" The carpenter smiled, showing a few missing teeth.

"Not at all. I was woolgathering. Norbert, right?"

"Aye."

"I was wondering if you could make me something."

The thought came again. Was she going to mess up history? Lucy fidgeted for a moment and then decided it was such a small thing, certainly it couldn't hurt. She picked up a twig, drawing in the dirt.

"It's called a crochet hook. Not very big, but the little hook on the end is important."

"How big around is the hook?" Norbert scratched his beard and Lucy swore she saw something jump to the ground. Yuck.

"The length is the same as my hand. The width about half of my little finger." She held up the finger in question to show him. "The hook is like this." She drew in the dirt again and picked up a small twig to show him how thick it should be.

"Aye, I can fashion such a tool. May I ask the use?"

"You use it with yarn to make things." Seeing his blank look, she continued, "You know, like washcloths, hats, gloves, scarves and sweaters."

"Like a weaver fashions clothing?"

She nodded.

Norbert blinked a few times. "As you say, mistress. I shall have it for you in a day." He still looked a bit confused, but she'd see what he came up with.

"How much will it cost?" She hoped it wasn't much, considering she didn't have a lot left over from her market day purchases.

The carpenter turned around. "Lord Blackford provides what I require. I will inform the steward in my accounting of the items I have fashioned."

"Great. I'll make you a scarf."

He looked dubious but smiled nonetheless. "Much obliged, my lady."

Happy, she went into the kitchens to check on the stew for dinner.

Lucy sent the serving boys out with the stew and garlic bread. She was looking forward to enjoying a glass of wine with dinner.

She came to a dead stop in the hall. It sparkled. There were new rushes and herbs scattered over the floors, the cobwebs and dirt gone. Fires blazed, the candles cast everyone in a flattering light and the minstrels from the market played softly.

Bertram stood before her. "May I escort you, mistress?"

She hugged him tight. "The hall looks amazing. It's lovely and smells so nice."

The man blushed.

"However did you do all this in one day? You could command armies."

He blushed some more. "I thank you."

Lucy took his arm. She sat next to him at dinner. After enjoying three meals cooked by her, the few men who crossed themselves when they passed her had quit doing so.

"'Tis a fine meal, my lady," one of the knights said.

Others joined in.

She glowed from all the appreciative comments. Even Clement the pig couldn't ruin her mood. Lucy leaned over to Bertram. "I cannot wait to see what you do with the rest of the castle."

The man grinned at her, patting his ample belly. "And I cannot wait to taste your next meal."

The music started up again and one of the knights asked her to dance. The only thing missing from the night being perfect? Dancing with William. She missed his scowls and grumbles. And she wondered, did he still think she was crazy for telling him she was from the future, or might he come around and believe her? It meant a great deal to her that he would believe her. Lucy danced with all of the men until she was out of breath.

She'd put down her mug of wine when another man approached. The smile fell off her face when she turned.

"Clement."

"I would be honored, my lady." He took her arm and led her to the makeshift dance floor. Well, he was a good dancer, she'd give him that much. Just when she thought they'd have a pleasant time, he narrowed his eyes.

"You have bewitched the men."

She stepped on his foot. Hard.

"I will stop you, witch. William will burn you or risk losing all."

"You are so handsome yet so ugly inside," she said sweetly.

Chapter Seventeen

Three long days in the rain to York. William would be grateful to spend the night in a nice, dry inn. After the nonsensical story Lucy had told him, William made the decision not to tell her he'd heard tale of a shipwreck from a distant land. One survivor. Other than her. If she was indeed from the shipwreck, which he doubted.

The Wolf's Ear Inn was a modest inn boasting fine stables. He tossed the reins to the stable boy. "Feed and water the horses."

The proprietor wiped his hands on an apron, smiling cheerfully. "Welcome, my lord. Will you be wanting dinner?"

"Aye, rooms and food, if you please."

Their cloaks steamed as they dried next to the fire. The proprietor's wife brought tankards of ale and platters of meat and bread.

"I fought alongside you many years, William. Why are we talking to the survivor of a shipwreck?"

His captain had fallen under Lucy's charm, as had most of the men at the castle. William wanted to believe her…a fantastical tale, no doubt. 'Twas easier to believe she hit her head and addled her mind.

"The lady desired to return home. I will aid her if I can."

His captain's face filled with doubt. "She is not Georgina. The lady is pleasant and kind. A match for you, William. Maybe 'tis time to remarry. Have children."

"I know she is not Georgina, but she is not telling the truth regarding how she came to be at Blackford." He shifted in his seat. "Until I know the truth, I do not trust her. I dare not."

His captain leveled a long look at William before turning back to his meal and digging in with gusto. He would feel better after a full belly and a good night's sleep.

Lucy filled her morning pulling weeds in the overgrown garden and making a mental list of the plants she needed. An herb garden, fruit trees, vegetables…and flowers, because they provided a bit of pretty in an otherwise functional garden.

Many of the villagers brought plants and seeds. Gave them a good excuse to get a good look at her. They'd be disappointed the fearsome Lord Blackford was not in residence. The gypsy woman was nowhere to be found when she'd looked for her at the market. With the speed gossip traveled, she had no doubt the woman would find her in due course.

A shadow fell over her, a raven soared overhead and when she looked up, a tiny old lady stood in front of her, waiting. It was as if she'd conjured the gypsy out of thin air. The woman had long silver hair braided down her back. Piercing brown eyes looked out of a face full of wrinkles, attesting to the fact she'd enjoyed a happy life.

"You seek information."

It was a statement made with a Mona Lisa smile. Lucy stood, wiped the dirt from the side of her face and just barely resisted the urge to squirm. "Would you like something to drink?"

When the woman nodded, Lucy had the feeling she had passed some kind of test. A wide-eyed Albin ran to the kitchens with instructions to fetch ale and the apple tarts she'd made early this morning.

Thomas frowned at the woman but refrained from saying anything, instead choosing to pace back and forth around the garden, occasionally casting an eye over the two of them. Talk about a man of few words. He was emulating William all too well. Lucy led her guest to a sheltered bench nestled in a corner of the garden.

She wasn't sure where to start, so she plunged right in. "The girls in the village say you provide love potions and things."

The gypsy woman turned a shrewd eye on her. "You have no need of a love potion." The woman's bracelets rattled as she moved her arms. Her heavy gold hoop earrings gently swayed in the breeze. She looked like a little peacock in the brightly colored peasant top and skirt. Like Lucy had picked a picture out of an old book of fairy tales.

Nothing ever ended well in those old stories. Most of the village women feared the gypsy but still went to her seeking help.

Albin brought the refreshments, chewing industriously as he approached, making Lucy bust out laughing.

"I see you ate a few of the tarts along the way." The boy's face fell. She patted him on the shoulder. "Don't worry, you're not in any trouble. Growing boys need to eat."

He smiled up at her and set the tray down on the wall next to them. Albin went to stand by Thomas but made sure he was close enough to hear whatever they talked about. Lucy knew he listened at doors. Made himself invisible, knowing people tended to ignore small children. He was a wealth of information.

They sat in companionable silence eating the tarts and drinking a glass of ale. The woman belched, rubbed a hand across her lips and turned to Lucy, waiting.

"Could you help me find my way back home?"

The woman took her palm, tracing the lines, mumbling to herself.

"You traveled a great distance. Overcame hardship. Now you learn to hold true to your self again." The woman took Lucy's chin in her hands. Brown eyes assessing, measuring.

"How do you know you are not where you are meant to be?"

Lucy resisted the urge to roll her eyes. Wasn't it just like a fortuneteller to give a totally vague answer?

"So are you saying I can't go home? I'm stuck here in 1307?"

The woman remained unruffled, tracing the lines on Lucy's palms. She cocked her head, listening to some voice only she could hear then nodded. "If you truly desire to go whence you came, you will have the chance to do so. Know this. Some things are meant to be. Trying to change your fate doesn't always ensure your desires. Sometimes what you want is not what you need, child."

The woman drank another cup of ale then narrowed her eyes. Lucy followed her gaze to see what or whom she was watching, and grimaced. Clement was coming toward them.

"Beware that one. He wishes ill on all. Will do great harm unless you stop him." She stood up. "He calls you witch out of fear. Fear carries power. Beware."

And with that, she turned and hurried down the path so quickly that Lucy lost sight of her.

Clement made the sign of horns to ward off evil. "What was

the gypsy woman doing here? Were you seeking a love potion? To entrap William?"

"I don't believe in love potions. We were simply having a nice chat about the garden. She brought me some plants and herbs."

Clement looked like he wanted to say more, but someone called his name. With a scowl, he turned on his heel and stomped out of the garden, stopping to pet one of the dogs that roamed the estate.

She pondered what the woman had said. If Simon was right, she knew what Clement would do to William. Well, not exactly what he would do, but she knew what the outcome would be. It seemed to her she needed to be the one watching over William instead of the other way around.

Time passed quickly. The first day of fall would be here before she knew it. Not sure whether to believe the gypsy woman or not, Lucy decided every night she would go up to the battlements to see if she could go back home. Just to be safe.

Did she really want to leave?

As she wiped her hands on a piece of cloth, she smiled. Pretty soon she would have new clothes. An apron with pockets and a dress with pockets. She'd never cared much about clothes until now. And if she were honest, she was really hoping she'd have a chance to wear the blue velvet dress.

A rumbling sound made her turn, looking for the source. It seemed to be coming from above. She was knocked to the ground, her breath whooshing out. She heard Albin cry out. A large chunk of stone pinned his arm to the ground. The arm was twisted at an unnatural angle.

She heaved herself to her feet and ran over to him. "What happened?"

"I saw the stone fall from the battlements, my lady. I pushed you out of the way. The stone hit my arm. It hurts."

Thomas ran over, lifting the rock off the boy's arm. "I'll send for the healer."

"Thank you, Thomas. It looks like his arm is broken. Hurry."

Lucy frowned, looking up at the battlements. She thought she saw a figure duck back. Someone didn't like her. Was it Clement? She thought the men's dislike was harmless. Bertram had convinced her the pie was bad, not poisoned. Now she wondered if someone meant to do her serious harm.

The stone was meant to hit her on the head, and instead Albin was hurt. She was grateful he'd saved her. If that chunk of rock hit her on the head, she'd be dead. The boy was so brave. Trying not to cry, he was pale and sweating, his body trembling. She sat with him and rocked him back and forth, whispering in his ear.

"You were very brave. Like a knight saving a lady from danger. I'll make you some cookies."

He wiped a tear away to smile. "What are cookies?"

She brushed the damp hair away from his forehead. "You'll like them very much. They're even better than apple tarts." William better come back soon. She needed to warn him. Seemed both of them were in danger.

Chapter Eighteen

"There were no women on board? You are certain?" William asked the survivor from the shipwreck again. The man recounted a terrible storm, the ship breaking apart, men screaming as they died in the cold water.

The sailor, perpetually darkened from the sun, shook his head. "No. No women on board. Only captain and crew, my lord."

The man rubbed the stump where he'd lost his leg at the knee. "No sailing until my new wooden leg is fashioned."

Lucy Merriweather was not on the ship. A raven settled on the fence post watching them. The sailor nodded to the big black bird.

"Some say ravens are the keepers of secrets and memories." He looked from William to the bird and back again, shaking his head. "The raven has a message, my lord."

William resisted the urge to snort. What could a bird tell him? Mayhap he was losing his wits much like Lucy? The bird cawed again, giving William the unsettling thought the bird was indeed speaking to him.

A sense of calm, much like he experienced in battle, settled over him. He could not say how he knew, only that he did. Lucy told him the truth.

She was indeed from the future. Likely he should fear the knowledge of things that would come to pass, though he yearned to learn about her time. She said something about a curse? Blackford would stand in her time, though in a ruinous state.

It saddened him to know all his efforts would be for naught. Did he leave no heirs? Had he truly never remarried?

The land called him home. How quickly he had come to care for Blackford and its inhabitants. Once home, he would talk with Lucy. Ask her to tell him more about things to come. Have her tell him about this curse.

How could he aid her? He could protect her with his body. His sword. And with his title. But he had no heavenly powers to send her through time to the future. He was having a difficult time believing such things were possible. Truth settled over him like a well-worn cloak, and he knew it to be true, no matter how difficult to believe.

Had God sent her back for him? The thought crossed his mind that he could spend the rest of his life with her and be happy. Just as quickly, he pushed the thought aside. Future or not? He would not take her as his wife.

Shelter and a place to live was all he could offer. He would see her settled however she desired. In truth, he did not want her to leave Blackford. She had become a part of the place. Even now he yearned to go home to her. Heard her laugh across the distance.

Back at the inn, the horses were saddled and waiting. Wymund stood talking softly to his mount. "Find what you were looking for, my lord?"

"I believe so." William settled into the saddle. "We make for home."

The healer set Albin's arm. He was very brave and Lucy fussed over him. Then the fever started. She moved him into her bedroom and spent the night and next day sitting up with him, worrying. Albin made her laugh, trailed her everywhere. She'd become attached very quickly.

He cried out in his sleep. Cried for his family. Lucy knew the feeling well. Such a brave boy. He never complained, never talked about home. Always cheerful and ready to help. It was nice to be in her own room. The men helped Lucy switch rooms with William so he could have his chamber back. She'd hogged his room long enough. And hers was pretty with the new chair, tapestry on the wall and a carpet Bertram found in one of the storerooms.

The view looked out over the water. With the shutters open, the breeze carried away the smell of sickness and filled the room with fresh air. The men were horrified she'd leave the window open, but chalked it up to her foreign ways and left her alone.

Thomas opened the door and one of the boys came in bearing a tray. "Bertram sent me with some porridge, my lady." A wistful look on his face, he said, "Will you be cooking again soon, mistress? We miss your food."

Lucy resisted the urge to laugh. She'd been so worried about Albin she hadn't cooked any meals for the men. Bertram told her not to worry, and went back to his old duties while continuing to supervise the cleaning of the castle from top to bottom.

What he'd been able to accomplish in a week was nothing short of amazing. The entire place practically sparkled. He was like a drill sergeant barking orders, ensuring everything was kept up to his standards.

William would be so surprised. She wondered again when he would return. Tomorrow, if she figured right. A week of missing him. Lucy laid a hand on Albin's forehead. Did he feel a bit cooler?

He opened his eyes. "I'm hungry."

"You gave us all quite a scare. You had a terrible fever." She picked up the bowl of porridge and helped him sit up in bed. His little arm was in a sling. He'd heal quickly and be back to his usual rambunctious self in no time.

Albin swallowed the porridge, making a face. "You didn't make this."

"No, Bertram was kind enough to cook while I stayed with you."

Albin touched her hand. "I know you're not my mother, but I thank you for caring for me." He looked at the porridge, a resigned look on his face, then opened his mouth. "I think you would make a good mother, mistress."

His words warmed her heart. "I did leave your side for a little while. But only to make you some cookies."

Lucy stood, went over to the small table next to the chair by the fire and brought back the basket. She pulled back the cloth, watching his eyes grow big.

"Are those for me?"

She touched his forehead once more, filled with gratitude he was going to be okay.

"Finish your porridge and you can have a cookie." He gave her such a sad puppy-dog face she grinned. "Eat it all and you can have two."

The boy ate his porridge and eagerly took both cookies.

With limited supplies on hand, Lucy did the best she could,

coming up with a basic sugar cookie. A look of sheer bliss filled his face as he chewed.

"I believe the angels have taken me to heaven." He ate the next cookie as quickly as the first, looking longingly at the basket.

"Oh no. I want to see you eat a good dinner then you can have another one tonight."

She stood and stretched out the kinks in her back. "My mama used to call me a greedy Gus when I ate all the sweets." Lucy wiped a crumb from his lip. "Don't worry, I made some for the others."

He licked his fingers and fidgeted in the bed. She knew she wouldn't be able to keep him there much longer. Best to pick your battles.

"Stay in bed until morning, then you can get up and run around again." She paused. "Do as I say, greedy Gus, and you can eat the rest of the cookies in the basket."

It probably wasn't the best thing to bribe a small child, but she'd work with the tools at her disposal.

As they rode, William thought about everything Lucy had told him. If she did know the future, in but a score of years his king would no longer reign. His sire would die a terrible death.

A queen on the throne of England? Mayhap a woman could rule the country. Many females ran estates while their husbands were off warring. 'Twas a strange notion, to be sure.

Lucy said people no longer rode horses. Instead riding in a metal carriage that didn't require beasts to travel. And traveled great distances in one day. He couldn't imagine such a contraption.

He looked up at the sky. People flying through the heavens. In metal sky carriages to other countries in mere hours. Why would she want to stay in his time when such wondrous things existed?

William gripped the reins, making the horse shake its head. Men walking on the moon. He cast his eyes heavenward. 'Twas not possible. Was it?

She spoke of things he couldn't fathom. And the curse. He needed to know what it spoke of. If there was a way to avoid the danger and protect his men and his home. He could not fail. Blackford would stand intact for generations.

As William and his men neared the border of his lands, a group of ruffians appeared out of the trees. An arrow hit him in the arm. He swore, jumping off his horse.

With the swing of his sword, he took out the first man. His men quickly engaged the others. The last man dropped his bow and ran. Wymund was after him. He knocked the man to the ground and dragged him back to William.

"Why do you attack us?" William growled at the man.

Wymund leaned down. "You know Lord Blackford. His reputation is legend. Speak now and he will grant you a quick death. Hesitate and he will make it long and painful."

The man whimpered. William shook him. The man sniveled, wiping his nose on a dirty sleeve. He held his hands up in front of his face. "Don't kill me, my lord. We was paid to attack you."

"Who paid you?"

The man started shaking. "I don't know, I wasn't there. My brother met him. The man was short and wore a hood to cover his face. He paid in gold, so we didn't ask questions."

Disgusted, William got to his feet. "Let him go. He is no threat to me."

The man got up and ran as fast as his legs could carry him. Wymund leaned in close so the others wouldn't hear. "There is a traitor amongst us."

With a curt nod, William said, "See what you can discover. Quietly."

The men mounted up and rode for the castle. A sense of urgency warned him to hurry. William had learned to trust his instincts. They'd kept him alive through many battles. Lucy needed him.

Blackford would defend against all threats. Threats outside and within. He knew those in the village whispered about him and his men even whilst seeking their protection. Soon in the distance he could see Blackford. More than seven hundred years would pass and the castle would stand. Pain lanced through him, and he wasn't sure if it was from where he'd pulled the arrow free from his arm or something else. Was it, mayhap, the thought that none of his bloodline would hold Blackford?

The following day Albin hopped out of bed, declared himself fit to guard Lucy and trailed her down the stairs and out to the gardens. Her ever-present shadow detached himself from the wall and followed her back inside to enjoy the main meal of the day. Lucy was starting to appreciate eating the biggest meal at lunchtime.

She wasn't used to manual labor. Spent all day sitting at a desk typing on a computer, with an occasional walk thrown in. And the gym? Forget it. Hated getting all sweaty and disgusting. But there was something about digging in the dirt with your hands, feeling the soil. Made you feel connected to the world around you.

Today she made sandwiches for lunch. Trenchers made of bread were used at meals, bread was wrapped around food and eaten at meals, therefore Lucy decided it wasn't too far-fetched to serve sandwiches.

Between working in the garden and cooking meals, she was exhausted. When she leaned against a corner of the wall in her room, a door opened with a creak. A secret passage filled with cobwebs and dust. Stairs led up to a tiny room at the top of a tower.

There were windows all around, and she fell in love with the space instantly. Bertram sent a couple of the men to clean, men he trusted. He said there were likely passages all over the castle, and Lucy made a mental note to talk to William. This afternoon she and a few others would continue exploring.

Her chaise would be perfect here. The carpenter should be done making it soon. She'd described to him what she wanted and he said he could make it. It would be perfect up here in this room with a table. One of the women she'd met in the village could sew. Lucy engaged her to make cushions for the chaise, along with some other things that were needed for the castle. The girl was young, and Lucy wanted to offer her a place here at Blackford. Clement had put his foot down and said no. The nosy pig. When William returned, she'd ask him.

She yawned and decided she could take a small nap before they started creeping through the walls.

Refreshed after an hour-long nap, Lucy spent about an hour exploring then was back in the garden. Her dress was filthy, so she took it off to be washed and found herself wearing William's tunic and hose again. At least everyone quit staring at her all the time. One of the men told her it was unsuitable for a lady, but she made a face and told him, "It's hot, I and my clothes are dirty, I don't have my new dresses yet and who can move around in a heavy dress anyway?"

He told her it was scandalous and she laughed. Told him, "You should see what they wear where I come from." She was still giggling to herself picturing the men visiting Holden Beach gawking at all the girls in bikinis when a shadow blocked out the light.

Chapter Nineteen

"I see you're wearing my clothes again." Seeing his tunic on her did something strange to his heart. When she looked up at him, William didn't know whether to bellow or hit something. He hauled her to her feet, shaking her so hard he swore he could hear her teeth rattle.

"Who did this to you?"

"You're hurting me." Lucy pulled away, wrapping her arms tight around herself.

"I'm glad to see you too, Godzilla," she said crossly. "When I was at the market in the village, someone pushed me. I tripped and kissed the ground with my face." She touched a finger to her face, where he could see the discoloration and a slight swelling on the left side around her lip. Rage coursed through him. William wanted to tear whoever had hurt her limb from limb. How dare someone touch her. She was under his protection. His.

She put a hand on his arm, the heat of her touch calming him instantly.

"It hurt like hell when it happened, but I'm fine."

Lucy took his arm and led him about the garden, pointing out all the plants and herbs she was growing. "Something else happened." She paused. "A piece of stone came loose from the battlements. If it wasn't for Albin, I'd most likely be dead."

He looked up in alarm, searching the walls for any sign of weakness. As if sensing his foul mood, she hurried to tell the rest of the tale.

"Albin pushed me out of the way. But in doing so, the stone landed on his arm. The poor kid broke his arm. He was so brave. You would be proud of him."

She twisted her hair through her fingers. He'd noticed she did it whenever she was thinking. William was mightily distracted by the sight.

"The child was in bed with a fever for two days. But he's back to his normal happy self and running around. Though his arm is in a sling. We sent for a healer from the village. She assured me he would heal without any problem."

She reached up, adjusting her hair. She tied it up with a piece of green ribbon, showing off her enchanting gray eyes. For a moment William wondered if she'd chosen the ribbon to remind her of him. He liked watching how her hair swayed back and forth when she walked. Just like her hips.

"I am heartened to know you both are well."

"Did you find what you were looking for?"

How to answer? William led her over to the stone bench and they sat down.

"I went to see a sailor. The only survivor from a shipwreck on a ship traveling from a faraway land." He looked at her, saw his words were not lost on her and continued.

"He assured me there were no women on board." William took her hand in his, marveling at the softness of her skin. Lucy was unused to hard labor. As most ladies were, but even highborn women tended to have marks on their skin from illness or other ailments. Lucy had none.

"I want to believe your tale."

She stood up, hands on her hips, shaking a finger at him. "Why is it so difficult to believe me? I told you the truth."

"Cease, woman." He ran a hand through his hair, calming himself before he spoke again. "I am trying to tell you I believe you. You must admit your story is wondrous." William pulled her back down. "What is a 'Godzilla'?"

She snickered. "A very large beast. Goes around stomping on things and breathing fire. Like you when you're mad."

He grinned, taking her hand in his and inhaling the scent of sunshine that seemed to follow her wherever she went. At first William thought it was the soap she used to bathe herself every day. Albin confided to him in awed tones how Lucy heated water in her chamber and washed every day. The child hated to wash. He'd hide from Lucy, and only gave in when she threatened to give his dessert to one of the other boys. William came to accept that the smell of sun and grass was her natural scent.

"I am sorry for all you have lost. To be so far from home, knowing there is no horse, no cart or ship to take you where you need to be. The grief of losing those you care for." He hesitated. "The man we found on the rocks? Was he your husband in truth?"

"Have you ever lost a battle? You're great at sneak attacks."

He didn't know why she asked, but he answered anyway. "No, but methinks I might today, lady."

Lucy laughed. "The story I told you is true. Simon was my boyfriend..." She saw the look on his face and elaborated. "He was wooing me. I came to England with him hoping the way we felt about each other would change. But I realized it would never change. He wasn't the right guy for me. We are who we are."

She looked off into the distance as if she could see her home if only she tried hard enough. Then she leaned on his shoulder and William's heart swelled with happiness.

"I came to realize Simon was not the man I thought he was. He only pretended to care for me. I found out it was my name he wanted." Now she looked up at him, a question on her face.

"Before I tell you about the curse, let me finish the rest of the story."

Thomas approached. "My lord."

William stood and clapped the young man on the back. "You have done well watching over the lady, Thomas."

He stood back, measuring the man in front of him. Thomas would make a fine knight. "I have need of you."

The boy looked eager. "Will you guard our lady? We have a traitor amongst us."

Thomas looked curious but refrained from asking questions, and instead simply nodded. "It will be my honor to watch over the lady."

He turned on his heel and made for the kitchens, calling over his shoulder, "I'll fetch some ale. You must be thirsty from your journey, my lord."

"I'm sorry. I didn't even think to ask if you'd been inside yet. Have you?"

She sounded curious, and it made William wonder what he would find in his hall.

"What's inside?" He stopped himself. "No, wait. Tell me the rest of the story then we'll go see what you have wrought in my hall."

"I want to know about this traitor, but it can wait until I finish the story." Lucy said. "As I was telling you, I came to England with Simon to visit his family home. Blackford Castle." She bit her lip.

"He proposed marriage but I said no. I thought I would go home the next day. But it seemed he had other plans."

William could see the distress on her face. He pulled her close, wanting to comfort her. Not saying a word, he kept silent, letting her tell him what she needed.

"That night he asked me if I would pretend to marry him. He said it would be fun and, trying to be nice, I agreed."

She looked at him, her eyes shimmering with tears, but they did not fall. "I know it was stupid, but I felt bad for ending the relationship, and I thought it would be make-believe. But it wasn't."

Lucy pressed her lips so tight together William watched them turn white. "He had a dress and everything arranged."

Her eyes narrowed and she clenched her fists. "Simon drugged my champagne." She hesitated. "Like a poison. I didn't know where I was or what I was doing. I married him for real. Though I never meant to. I thought it was a game."

He could feel the tension in her body as she leaned against him. Hear the beating of her heart as he thumped her on the back.

"The next thing I remember, there was a terrible storm. I was outside on the battlements wearing my wedding dress…" She sniffed but did not cry. William thought she might not swing a sword, but she was as strong as any warrior he had known.

"The man I thought I loved."

Jealously raged through him at the thought she loved another.

"But it was never love. It was the silly infatuation of a girl. I know that now. Simon tried to push me over the battlements. He hit me. I remember his hands around my neck." She shuddered.

"A great crack of lightning hit as he threw me over the edge. There were terrible sounds and such darkness. When I woke up it was morning and your men were standing over me." Lucy stared off into the distance.

"At first I couldn't make sense of what I was seeing. And Simon was nowhere to be seen. You have to understand." She looked up at him, and the anguish in her eyes undid him.

"He told me he made sure my sisters would be murdered. You see, he didn't want them coming to look for me. One thing about Simon, he always accomplished what he set out to do. I know in my heart they are dead. And I could do nothing to stop it."

After this truth, a single tear spilled down her face. William caught it on his fingertip, watching it glisten in the sunlight.

He took her face in his hands and kissed her. Thoroughly.

"Pardon, my lord." Albin stood before them, a grin on his small face. Lucy's face turned a fetching shade of pink. William was happier than he had been in…well, in a very long time.

She sat with a dazed look on her face, fingertips touching her lips. William's male pride swelled.

"How is your arm, my young warrior?"

The boy smiled, telling the tale of how he had saved the lady from certain doom.

"You have guarded her well. Would you like to be part of the lady's personal guard?"

Albin's eyes shone with excitement. "Yes, my lord. I will keep her safe." He shifted from foot to foot, clearly impatient. "Will you come see the hall?"

William ruffled the boy's hair. "Allow Lucy to finish telling me her tale and then I will come see the wonders of my hall."

Albin grinned and ran toward Thomas, no doubt to tell him of his promotion. Thomas would make a fine captain of Lucy's guard. It wasn't as if she could get back to her future, so she would need her own men to watch over her.

Or could she still go back? Might she leave him?

He thought not. She had been here this long. He and some of the men had watched her perform her mysterious rituals atop the battlements. He knew now she was trying to return to her own time. But she could not. William shouldn't feel joy at the revelation. But he did. Wanted her for himself. Georgina be damned.

"Now the curse. And then you need to tell me about this traitor. I know they are linked." Lucy patted his arm, looked at the red on her hand and leapt to her feet. "Why didn't you tell me you're bleeding?"

He looked down to see a small pool of blood by his feet. "'Tis naught but a scratch. Worry not, my lady." William pulled her down onto his lap. "Tell me the rest of your story. You'll feel better once you finish."

"Simon had a strange notion. He said my last name wasn't really Merriweather. That I wasn't Lucy Merriweather. I was Lucy *Brandon.*"

She felt his surprise, for she nodded. "You had the same reaction as me."

Lucy bit her lip and went on. "Brandon is your last name. Now you know why I was so surprised when I found out." She shifted to get comfortable in his lap, and William wanted to curse.

"Remember what I told you? Simon said his ancestor took Blackford Castle by force from a traitor to the crown in 1307. He said the Grey family had held it ever since. Clement's last name is Grey."

William didn't know what to say. So many thoughts ran through his mind. He knew there was a traitor amongst them. Now she told him he would lose his castle this very year. He hadn't believed her before.

"Bloody hell. Isn't that what you like to say when you're mad?" Lucy slid off his lap and stood in front of him, frowning. "Obviously you are Lord Blackford. You are the accused traitor to the crown. Clement is the one behind all of this. The only question is why?"

And wasn't that the question? "Ladies shouldn't swear," he said, a smile on his face.

She snorted and stuck her tongue out at him. "Should I stomp around, bellowing and yelling like you?"

He couldn't help it: William threw back his head and laughed. It felt good to laugh. What would he do if she left him? It seemed he now had a traitor to root out.

"Stop scowling and come into the hall and see all the changes." Lucy looked happy and full of excitement as she pulled him to his feet. Then she let go. "I'm sorry, we should see to your arm first."

"'Tis only a scratch."

She rolled her eyes. "Yes, I know. You're the big, bad warrior. But we'll stop in the kitchens and take care of your arm first. You'll want to be prepared to see all the changes." She gave him a sly look. "And I have apple pie in the kitchen."

He felt as if he were preparing for battle as he went up the steps to his home. Ready to see womanly frippery decorating the hall and chambers, William envisioned lace and beads and a great deal of pink.

Chapter Twenty

William followed his nose into the kitchen, seeking out Lucy. He patted his belly.

"I have never eaten chicken prepared in such a manner. What do you call it again?"

The entire kitchen smelled of honey as Lucy leaned over a cauldron, sniffing the concoction brewing inside.

She turned around to smile at him, and he noticed the heat from the fire had turned her cheeks a fetching shade of pink.

"Fried chicken. With mashed turnips and parsnips." She handed him another one of the delicious desserts she called sugar cookies.

The cookie disappeared in two bites. "The green weeds with walnuts, apple and crumbled cheese?"

"You liked the salad? I made the dressing from mustard and oil and spices."

He grimaced. "I would not venture to say I enjoyed the greens. The men were grumbling and poking at the pile as if it would bite them."

Lucy laughed. The sound filling the kitchens and filling his heart. "Yes, but they ate it, didn't they?"

"The men knew they must finish your salad. They wanted sugar cookies for dessert. You have spoiled us all. We'll all turn to fat."

She grinned. "Then I guess you won't want to taste what I'm making?" She stirred in crumbs from the bread then turned back to face him. "You can all go fight with each other out in the lists. Work off what you ate for dinner and dessert."

William sniffed. Smelled good in here. "Mayhap a small taste," he said nonchalantly, as if he really didn't care. When in truth the curiosity was killing him.

"It's ginger candy, or maybe gingerbread? I'm not really sure what it's called. But I remember the recipe."

She sat down at the table. William poured a cup of wine for her and a mug of ale for himself. Perhaps she was becoming accustomed to his time. She smiled more, and he hoped the sadness weighing her down would lift.

So he could watch the expressions on her face, William sat across from her. She moved her hands when she spoke with her soft lilt.

"You know the hives in the gardens?"

He thought for a moment. "The monks brought them from the abbey. Be careful of the gypsy woman. Many fear her."

"I didn't tell her I was from the future…though she seemed to know."

"I made a donation of gold to the abbey."

She smiled. "I sent one of the men to deliver scarves I crocheted for the monks to thank them for the bees. I adore honey."

One of the youngest boys went over to the pot and dipped a spoon in. "Martin. No more honey until it's done." She ruffled his hair and shooed him out of the kitchen. William could see her as mother to a child.

"So I boiled the honey then I added some spices."

He sniffed. "Ginger and cinnamon?"

"And pepper and saffron. Then the breadcrumbs."

'Twas good he had plenty of gold, as much as she'd spent on spices and wool. William noticed everyone seemed to receive one of her scarves or hats. Too warm to wear now, but soon the men would wear her gifts.

"After you stir in the breadcrumbs it makes everything thick. Let it cool slightly then pour it onto a flat surface and make it into a rectangle." She motioned with her hands. "Once it's cooled, we cut it into squares, put a clove in each square and eat it." Her eyes twinkled and he found her enthusiasm infectious.

"Where's young Albin? I expected to find him at your heels. The boy has developed quite a taste for sweets." And a strong attachment to the lady sitting across from him. As had all the men in his care.

She leaned back in the chair and took another sip of her wine. "I sent him into the wine cellar." She raised her eyebrows at him. "Did you know you have a wine cellar?"

William knew now. Thomas and Albin had discovered it while exploring the secret passages in the castle.

"The men said there are many bottles of spirits." He would have to make sure they weren't down there drinking up the entire storeroom. Best put a guard on the door for a while.

"Well, I'm glad there's wine down there. I've developed a taste for the stuff."

He looked at her curiously. "Did you not drink wine...where you come from?"

William stretched his legs out in front of him. The kitchen was warm. He could hear sounds of the men moving around in the hall, the guards calling out as they changed shifts. A comforting scene. All that was missing were children running around. He hadn't thought he would ever have children. Not after Georgina.

"At home we drink water and tea. And a most wondrous drink called Pepsi." A look of bliss spread across her face. For a moment William found himself jealous of a drink. "Y'all don't drink water often?"

"In some places the water is bad. The well here is deep, the water clear and sweet. My men and I drink it. But usually people drink wine or ale. Even small children drink watered-down ale with meals."

"Water is good for you."

He pondered this.

Wymund came into the kitchen. "My lord? A word?"

William stood, hauled Lucy across the table and kissed her. He found whenever he was around her he wanted to kiss her senseless. Make her his own.

"I am in debt to you for all you have done." William gestured around the room, meaning the castle in general. "Bertram is content ordering the men around."

"Don't we all like to order others around?" Lucy said. And Wymund chuckled.

"You can order me about, lead me around by my nose and whisper sweet words to me. Just don't tell the men." William kissed her again, gratified to hear her feminine laugh.

Wymund made a face as they walked out of the kitchen. "You must tell her before she hears the story from someone in the village."

William chose to ignore his captain. After hearing her tale about the man she called Simon, if he told her about Georgina, she would run as fast as far as she could. Just like all the others.

In his chamber, William paced back and forth in front of the fire. She'd been sleeping in his bed. While grateful to have his room back, he wondered what it would be like to share a chamber with Lucy.

The changes she'd made in his absence suited Blackford. From the chairs in front of the fire in the hall to the tapestries on the walls and fresh-smelling herbs scattered amongst the rushes on the floor. He admired the womanly touches, even the flowers. There were flowers in a mug on the table in the hall, on the worktable in the kitchen and in his room. He'd even found flowers in a mug in his solar and garderobe this morn.

He could get used to having her around. William shut the door behind him and went down to the solar to go over the ledgers with Clement.

When he walked in, the man sat in his chair, feet propped up on the desk.

"William. I hear you were attacked on the road home."

For the first time in his life, William felt suspicion take root as Clement spoke.

"I am unharmed. The ruffian's dead." He stood looking at his friend, who reluctantly vacated the seat and moved to take a chair next to the desk. William sat down, stretching his legs out in front of him.

"We caught one of the men." Was it a look of fear that crossed Clement's face? "The man said he was hired to kill me. And my men. There is a traitor amongst us. What have you heard?"

Clement sat up straight. "Aye, there is a traitor. The mistress

Lucy."

"You no longer call her witch?"

Clement should have known William well enough by now to hear the anger in his voice. He didn't meet William's gaze. "No. I have come to my senses. She is not a witch. But we know nothing of her. Her strange manner of speech. I have sent inquiries. No one knows her. She has no kin. Therefore she arrived to cause trouble. To turn you against me. My days are consumed with doing what is best for Blackford, my lord."

"If she is the one causing the trouble then why would someone try to harm her?"

Clement looked innocent. "What do you mean, my lord?"

William noticed Clement only called him "my lord" when he wanted to seem as if he was a servant. But he heard the disdain in the tone for the first time.

"Someone pushed her in the market. A stone almost landed on her. If it wasn't for Albin, the lady would likely be dead. I do not believe she is the one causing trouble. Someone else wishes her ill." William looked at Clement until the man looked away first.

"I will find out who means the lady harm. Whoever is harming her harms me. She is under my protection. I will see them dead."

Clement then spoke of the estate and matters requiring his attention. "Did you know the lady wants women to work in the castle? She wants them to live here," his steward said, incredulity filling his voice.

More likely, Clement wanted to pick them. He liked plump, lazy wenches, and Lucy would want women who would work as hard as she.

"I have decided to allow women in the castle." William held up his hand. "Not wenches. You can go to the village to meet your needs. But women to work. There is much to be done. A lady such as Lucy should not be cooking and cleaning."

It saddened William to think his childhood friend had turned against him. He would not act until he had proof the man he thought of as brother would commit such treachery.

Chapter Twenty-One

While the gingerbread candy cooled in the kitchen, Lucy relaxed in the tiny tower room and crocheted. She warned the men not to sneak any of the dessert. And if they did they wouldn't get any for a week. In fact, she told them she would give it all to Penelope, her favorite cow. She smiled remembering the looks of horror crossing their faces.

She picked a ball of yarn in a dark shade of brown. It would make the perfect scarf for Norbert. To repay him for making her the hook. The wood had a nice weight and was smooth in her hand. Since the yarn was chunky it should work up quickly and make a nice scarf. She'd chained one hundred and fifty stitches. It looked wide enough. She started to half double crochet when the door opened, making her jump. William ducked under the entrance, deftly scooping up the ball of yarn that went rolling across the floor. As he walked, he wound the yarn around the ball and handed it to her, leaning down for a quick kiss.

"You startled me. Is Thomas with you?"

Albin followed, coming over to touch the yarn in the basket. "He is in your room guarding the door, mistress."

"Albin and I have spent the morn exploring some of the passages. 'Tis easy for one to move through the castle unseen. There are spy holes in several of the rooms. Two of the men are sealing them up."

"Just be careful. Somebody has obviously been using the passages." She looked at Albin. "I would hate for anything to happen to you. Either of you."

He started to protest, and she raised a hand. "I know. You are a man and I should not worry. But I am a mere woman, therefore I worry over you." She caught the smile twitching at the corner of William's mouth.

Just then he seemed to notice the chaise she was stretched out on. He bent down, examining the cushion and the frame. "A reclining chair?"

"Yep. I call it a chaise." She stood up. "Try it."

William gingerly sat down in the chair then stretched out, sighing as he leaned back. "'Tis most comfortable."

"Oh, no you don't. That's my chair. I'll have Norbert make one for you."

"The carpenter fashioned this?"

"He did. And a girl from the village made the cushions." She held up her crochet hook. "He also made me this."

William took the hook from her. "This is the tool you use to fashion your gifts?"

Albin jumped up and down. "It's called a crochet hook. The lady made me a scarf. You wrap it around your neck to keep you warm in the winter. She's making this one for Norbert. Then Thomas, and then I guess she'll make you a present. If you're very nice to her."

William smiled at the boy, and Lucy laughed. "I would like to learn how to spin wool. Do you think one of the girls from the village could do it here? I was thinking we could have some of the girls clean, help in the kitchens, wash and other things as needed. Maybe one more to help me in the garden?"

William reluctantly gave her back the comfortable chair. "'Tis very soft."

"It's stuffed with goose feathers."

He looked thoughtful. "We should have geese."

As he opened the door to leave, he turned back. His look promised more kisses later when Albin wasn't around. "It's time to allow women in the castle. You are a lady. You should not be doing such chores. Send for whatever help you need."

The next morning Lucy busied herself making omelets and French toast. The men had told William about their new favorite breakfast. He wanted to try the dish. She would have to make sure to teach the girls how to cook her new dishes.

As she sent the last serving boy out with the platters of food, Albin crept into the kitchen.

Lucy covered her nose. "Oh my stars, what is that stench?"

Albin looked dejected. He was covered in some kind of brown sludge, and the smell wafted off him. She covered her nose, trying to breeze through her mouth.

"Mistress, it's shite."

"So early in the morning?" She wrinkled her nose. "How on earth did you end up covered in poop?"

He stood dripping on the floor as Lucy called for two of the men to fill up the bathtub in the small room off the kitchen.

"The boy who empties the barrels under the chutes…"

"What chutes?" Lucy was confused. What was he talking about?

Albin reached out to take her hand, seemed to think better of it and let the hand drop by his side, droplets of poop splattering onto the floor.

"If you'll follow me, mistress. I'll show you."

Lucy wanted to get outside and breathe in the fresh sea air, so she followed the boy out and around the corner of the castle. She hadn't been to this far corner before, and as they got closer, she smelled a terrible stench. Like sewage.

She could see a barrel and, as she looked up, a hole in the stone.

Albin pointed to the hole. "That's one of the garderobes. When you go, it comes out here." He pointed to the barrel.

"How utterly disgusting." She put her hands on her hips and looked at him. "You dripped poop all over my clean kitchen floor. If I hadn't already asked the men to fill the tub, I'd send you down to the water to bathe."

"I can't swim."

"It's probably too cold to go swimming anyway. When it's warm next summer, I'll teach you how to swim." She was talking as if she'd be here then—and then realized. She wanted to be here. Lucy thought of Blackford Castle as home. She loved Albin as she would a brother.

And William. They'd done nothing more than kiss. The relationship with him was the slowest she'd ever taken things, and it felt right to go slow. Get to really know someone before you created false intimacy by jumping in the sack.

Oh heavens. She was falling hard for her knight in tarnished armor. She only hoped he would turn out to be the man she thought he was. For if he wasn't, this time her heart would break into a million pieces and never recover.

She clapped her hands together. "Inside. And into the tub."

"I hate to bathe."

"Do you want a piece of ginger candy?"

The boy's shoulders slumped as he dragged his feet, slowly making his way into the kitchen as if he were marching to his death. Lucy tried not to laugh, she really did, but a single giggle escaped. Then another and then she couldn't stop.

"I'm sorry. I'm not laughing at you. I've never seen someone covered in poop before. It's exactly as I would have imagined."

He gave her a baleful look and stomped into the room off the kitchen.

"Leave your icky clothes in a pile by the tub. You're going to wash them after you're done. I'm not touching them."

"It wasn't my fault. I didn't start it," Albin said from the other room.

"I don't care who started it. When you see the boy next, tell him to come see me." Little boys liked to talk trash to each other. Lucy figured it would work itself out. But as the men were treating her as lady of the castle whether she wanted it or not, she decided she better hand out some kind of punishment. William would likely spank the boys, and that would humiliate them.

Though in her mind it was punishment enough having to empty barrels full of pee and poop. Yuck.

A few days later an assortment of girls and women stood in front of her. William insisted she add a lady's maid to the growing list of workers. With signs pointing to a rough winter, people wanted to be here. The castle would provide steady food and shelter.

She saw the men and several of the women eyeing each other. With a smile, she thought there would be several weddings taking place soon enough.

As she set the girls to their duties, she thought about her conversation with William. A guard of her own. Thomas would be her captain and Albin would serve her as well. William told her they would answer to her and her alone. Of course, he said, they all answered to him. To which she'd retorted, "Oh yes, great Lord Blackford." At that he threw back his head and laughed.

"Arrogant much?"

To which he only laughed louder.

"My lady?"

One of the girls in the kitchen held a jar in her hand. Mary was her name. She was going to show Lucy how to make homemade toothpaste. She'd been using a twig to scrub her teeth, but they always felt kind of scummy. And now that a certain handsome and sometimes cranky lord was kissing her, she wanted to make sure she didn't have bad breath.

The girl looked through the supplies in the kitchen and placed flour, honey, something called alum and mint on the table. She showed Lucy how she mixed everything together then put it in a small pot.

"Dip the twig in the mixture and scrub your teeth with it, my lady."

"Thank you so much for showing me how to make the tooth powder."

The girl blushed, looking down at her feet before shyly looking up at Lucy. "I have heard the men talking about your ginger candy. Would you show me how to make it?"

"I'd love to. The men have developed quite a taste for the stuff." She leaned toward the girl and said in a mock whisper, "If you want them to do something for you, simply tell them you won't give them any unless they do what you ask." The girl looked full of wonder with possibility and then grinned. Lucy wondered if she had her eye on Thomas. He'd be a good catch. Now she was happy she wanted everyone paired off.

Clement lounged in the third-best chamber in the hall and sulked. He spent the day inspecting the work as it progressed on the castle. The masons and carpenter were making good progress. When Blackford was his he would be a good and fair ruler.

Clement patted the dog sleeping next to his feet. "All the scraps you can eat, boy."

He checked to make sure the bar was secure across the door and the passage leading out of his room was empty. That runt of a boy, Albin, liked to lurk about. To be safe, he left the door to the passage cracked open so he would hear anyone sneaking about.

The passages had served him well. One night soon after his arrival he was in his cups. Making his way to the chamber, he fell against the wall and was shocked when it opened and he fell down a few steps into a dusty corridor.

Clement cursed. Now William knew about the passages. He and the men were busy exploring. Though he hadn't found them all. Clement snorted. If only he'd found the one leading down to the wine cellar. His time in exile at Blackford would have been much more pleasant.

The fire provided enough light for him to write a letter. A forged letter from William to Robert the Bruce. In the letter William said the new king was weak. He would not support a weak king. He expressed his wishes to change sides and support the Bruce. Provide gold to support his efforts to win Scotland's independence.

Satisfied with the letter, he sat back and envisioned all the changes he would make when the castle was his. Clement would send a messenger to the king with the letter. The messenger would say the letter had been discovered by Clement. And William would be tried for treason. The king would show his gratitude and award Clement Blackford Castle, the title and William's substantial gold.

Satisfied with the plan, Clement called to his man outside the door.

"Send for a messenger. 'Tis urgent."

Clement drank his ale and thought about his childhood friend. All their lives William was the favorite. Better with sword, faster on a horse and more skilled in battle.

Once he was thrown in the tower awaiting execution, Clement would tell him who he really was. What they were to each other.

Mayhap he would take Lucy for his bride. Though he would need to beat her every day. She had a sharp tongue when she was displeased. He would enjoy beating her. And getting her a fat belly. A babe of his own. He would love the child, make sure everyone knew the babe was his. His son would never feel unwanted or unloved. Happy thoughts filling his mind, he fell asleep in front of the fire.

Chapter Twenty-Two

Albin hopped up and down. "Come, mistress."

"Where are we going?"

Lucy finished showing two of the girls how to make French toast. She wiped her hands on her apron and sent up a word of thanks to the seamstress. Pockets were so practical. She'd never given them a second thought in her own time. Taken them for granted. She'd taken a lot for granted.

Like having clean clothes that fit. The dress she wore was a dark brown with embroidery around the hem and sleeves. The flowers stitched in gold. The cream-colored apron made a nice contrast, and she'd put her hair in a bun, using the beautiful jeweled pins William gave her as a gift.

Albin reached under the worktable for a large basket. "We're going down to the cove. You said we could eat lunch outside." He looked around the kitchen, grabbing a wheel of cheese.

"You go ahead. I'll pack our lunch and be along shortly."

Back home, she would have walked across the street to the ocean and spent the whole day lazing in the sun. Even in the fall there would be a few warm days before the weather turned cold for good.

When she woke now it was cold in the morning. Lucy reached up, touching fingertips to her lips. She and William had been inseparable. He walked her to her room every night, kissed her good night then pushed her inside, closing the door. Some nights she heard him pacing back and forth before he went to his own chamber.

It was nice not to worry about him having expectations. Wanting more than she was willing to give right away. Everyone was in a hurry. Hurry and date, find a husband, hurry to work, hurry to activities. It was exhausting just thinking about the pace of life she'd left behind.

Lucy finished packing the picnic basket. Thomas appeared with blankets draped over his arm and a smile on his face. There were three other men behind him. Lucy shook her head. She still couldn't get over the fact she had her own personal guard.

A few nights ago William came back from riding with a long scratch down the side of his face. He told her a tree fell in front of them. When they looked at the tree it was obvious someone cut it to make it fall on purpose. So it seemed the mysterious traitor was still at work. Her money was on Clement. But since she couldn't prove it, she'd quit nagging William. He wasn't ready to believe his childhood friend would betray him. Not that she could blame him. But she'd found out the hard way how easy it was for one person to hurt another.

Thomas made that sound only men seemed able to form in the back of his throat. It told her he was annoyed that she was taking so long without him saying a word. Since ending up in medieval England, she'd found herself staring off into space thinking, a lot.

"I think that's everything. Let's go." She handed the baskets to the men and grabbed her cloak.

Outside, more men stood around fidgeting, waiting for her. They made a large group, and for a moment she wondered if she had packed enough to eat. Doing a few quick calculations in her head, she nodded. She'd over-packed but was certain they'd eat it all. The men could put away enormous amounts of food and still look like they'd spent all their time in a gym.

They made their way down to the sheltered cove. The sun was shining, and though the day was warmer than last week, Lucy shivered, the breeze off the water making her feel chilly. She wrapped the cloak more tightly around her and let William lead her over to a flat rock where he'd spread out a blanket.

"Did you swim in the sea…back home?

"I learned to swim when I was very small. We lived by the ocean."

"The place called Holden Beach?"

She handed him a few blackberries. After what had happened with Alan and Simon, she couldn't eat the berries at first. But her love for the delicious berries overcame her ick factor. They were almost gone and she would miss the taste. They tasted so different from the ones she'd eaten at home in North Carolina.

"Yes. My sisters and I loved to spend the day at the beach. But we dressed differently. People put on bathing suits—small pieces of cloth—and spend the day sitting in the sun and swimming in the water."

She saw the look on his face and started to laugh.

"You think it's scandalous when I wear your tunic and hose, you should see what people wear in my time."

She described a bikini to him and watched the looks cross his face. A couple of the men nearby were listening, and she could see them picturing all that bare skin on display.

"I cannot believe so many women walk around wearing so little," William said. He pulled her against a rock to block the wind. Then he rested his head in her lap. She ran her fingers through his dark brown hair. There were pieces the color of honey, some more golden and a few auburn. He had hair color a hairdresser would kill to recreate.

Albin explored the small tidal pools around the cove, occasionally running over to show them something he'd found. Some of the men dozed while the others kept watch.

"Ladies do not take husbands?" William sounded perplexed. "Who protects them?"

She thought about how to answer the question. "In my time ladies are equal to men. They hold jobs, make their own money, decide if they want to have children or not. Even if they want to marry or not."

She took his hand in hers, tracing the scars across the back.

"As to protection. Things are different. In some ways life is much easier. Women go to work in offices. They drive cars... The horseless carriages I told you about. And I was going to say they don't need protection."

Lucy stroked his cheek and touched his crooked nose. "But so many terrible things happen in my world. Maybe they do need protection."

"Do you miss your time terribly?" William asked softly.

His men were far enough away not to hear the conversation.

"There are some things I miss. Like the convenience of being able to go into a shop and buy any kind of food you want, no matter the season. Movies and books and music. But most of all I miss my sisters and aunt. I guess it doesn't really matter what you have. Without family it's all meaningless."

They sat quietly, content to listen to the waves breaking against the rocks, the birds calling overhead and the men murmuring to each other. A curious seagull landed close to them, looked them over, then with a squawk took to the air, looking for better offerings.

"Do you have family? I've never heard you talk about them," Lucy said.

William shifted. She felt the hardness of his body, the tension running through him.

"I am all that is left of the Brandon name." He pulled her down and kissed her, as if fortifying himself before he went on. Lucy had a momentary pang of nerves as she wondered what he was going to tell her.

"My father and mother wanted many children. But my mother became ill soon after bearing me. Illness took from her the ability to give my father any more children. She was heartbroken. And my father never forgave her. He blamed her for the illness. In time he reconciled himself to the fact he only had one son, but he never treated her with the same care. She always seemed sad. My father, the Earl of Ravenswing, tried to be a good man. He died when I was ten and away fostering with another family. He was hunting and was gored by a boar. My mother died a year later." William looked down at Albin playing with a few of the other boys from the castle and smiled. "I always wanted brothers and sisters. Clement is the closest thing I have to a brother. So you can see why I am loath to blame him for the treachery here at Blackford."

Lucy held his hand. "I'm sorry you lost your parents at such a young age. I was also ten when my parents were killed in a sailing accident. My sisters, Charlotte and Melinda, we were all raised by Aunt Pittypat."

Lucy smiled thinking of her aunt. "My mother had two sisters. The three of them couldn't have been more different. My aunt Mildred, she was very proper. Never married. And we were always afraid to sit on the furniture."

The memories came back to Lucy so clear it was as if she were watching a movie.

"Aunt Pittypat raised my sisters and I." Lucy laughed, causing a few of William's men and her own guard to look over before they went back to keeping watch.

"Everyone here would call her a witch. She liked to dance outside by the light of the moon. She believes in ghosts and spirits and thought nothing of talking to my parents every day after their death." Lucy stared out over the water, picturing her aunt.

"Every Friday night we got to stay up all night and hang out with my aunt and her friends. She had the most interesting friends."

Lucy savored the warmth from William's body as the afternoon turned colder. "On our birthdays, she would wake us up in the middle of the night. We would get up and go down to the kitchen where we would have cake. We all liked a different kind of cake. Mine was angel food with cream cheese frosting."

Seeing the question on his face she said, "You like the sugar cookies I made? You would go to war for angel food cake with cream cheese frosting."

Knowing she'd never see any of them again brought the familiar pang of hurt, but today, for the first time, it wasn't so bad as to take her breath away. In time she hoped the pain would lessen to the point she could speak of them fondly without wanting to cry her eyes out.

"Would you tell me about your sisters?" William asked.

Albin ran over. "I'm hungry. Can we eat now?"

William laughed and sat up. "I think you will grow as tall as my knights as much as you eat, young Albin."

He called the men over and Lucy set out a picnic for everyone. "I'll tell you about Melinda and Charlotte tonight."

They passed a pleasant afternoon together. Getting to know each other better. Maybe she had been sent back because this was where she was supposed to be? Maybe the gypsy was right.

The minstrels moved on to another town, so it was quiet after dinner. Lucy sat in a chair in front of the fire with William beside her. With the basket of yarn in her lap she decided to make scarves for the rest of the villagers. It was relaxing to sit by the fire crocheting, listening to the men talking. Knowing William didn't expect anything of her. She didn't have to worry about how she looked or acted. He seemed to like her just the way she was.

Since William liked the scarf, expressed delight at how soft and warm it was, she decided to crochet him an afghan for Christmas.

Christmas. It was almost the first day of fall. And while she had tried to go home many more times, nothing ever happened. So maybe she was meant to be here for whatever reason. She was happy. Happier than she'd been in a very long time. Maybe the happiest she'd ever been.

She didn't know what would happen if she found out she could go home. Would she make the choice to leave? Would she stay here with the man she had fallen in love with?

Life in medieval England had a certain rhythm. One she was finding suited her perfectly.

Things were different in this time, though. She was a nobody and William was rich and titled. Would it matter if he married a nobody? Of course, it wasn't like he'd asked her or anything, she was just thinking.

Knowing he believed her, accepted her for who she was. It was enough. Lucy found herself looking forward to seeing him.

Wondering what he was doing when he wasn't with her. Was happy sitting next to him in companionable silence. Loved watching him train in the lists, seeing the smile on his face when he walked into a room and caught sight of her.

This was what a relationship was supposed to be like, she thought with a smile.

Chapter Twenty-Three

"My lord, 'tis time to question the steward. A messenger was seen leaving the castle with letters from Clement." Wymund stood before William, a grave look on his face.

"Clement sends many messages. He's trying to gain support to win back favor with the king and have his lands returned. A messenger coming or going does not mean he's plotting."

What was his childhood friend up to? Was it merely trying to win back his home, or something more unwholesome? Over the past several months he'd been watching Clement. Out of favor with the king meant he was also out of favor with many of the nobles. His pride damaged when he was banished from court, his friend now wanted only to whore, drink and sleep the day away. Naming him steward had not made matters better, only worse. But if he left Blackford, Clement would have nowhere to go. No one to take him in. William was his last hope. Mayhap 'twas why Clement didn't have the inclination to do anything else except eat through William's larder.

The thought of losing his title, lands and gold made William take a deep breath. How far would he be willing to go to win back what was his? He knew if he were Clement, he would never stop trying. Therefore, William would not condemn the man without proof.

Lucy said a man named Grey owned his castle in the future. The man told her his ancestor took the castle by force. William scoffed, imagining Clement trying to take the castle by force. Likely he would brandish a leg of mutton in one hand, a tankard of ale in the other and be distracted by a comely wench. No. It was not him. He would look to his borders. Discover which nobles wished him ill. Georgina's cousin inhabited a castle to the west. Close enough to Blackford that the earl could strike at him. He wanted William dead.

"Take a small contingent of men and scout the lands to the west. The earl may be making mischief."

"Yes, my lord. We will leave immediately. I have received word from the man I sent. The messenger is with his mistress enjoying her favors. We will find out what the letters are about." His captain turned to go then stopped.

"William?"

His captain rarely called him by his given name, though William had given him leave to do so after all they had been through together. He had a feeling he was not going to like what the man had to say.

"I've grown rather fond of mistress Lucy. With the number of women in the castle, she is bound to hear whispers."

He hesitated, clearly uncomfortable. "Tell her about Georgina. She should hear the tale from you, especially if her cousin is causing trouble."

William scowled. "I love her. I plan to make her my lady. There is no need to tell her about my wife."

Was he making the right decision in not telling her? After what she had been through with Simon, William knew she would leave him if she heard the tale.

He decided he would spend the rest of the day in the lists where things made sense. Striding into the courtyard, he passed Clement. "Care to join me in the lists?"

Clement made a face. "Nay, I have matters requiring my attention."

"As you wish." William's mood lifted as he inhaled the salty air. History changed as time passed. Mayhap events had not happened as Lucy thought. There were always plots afoot. This was a mere distraction. He would marry her, and they would have many children and be happy. A Brandon would live in Blackford in her time. He looked around, pleased with the work taking place. Blackford would not fall to ruin. It would stand and defend.

As his love for her would endure.

Lucy pulled on the wrist warmers she'd crocheted. They were a lovely heather-gray color. She loved the smell of fall. For a moment she wondered if she could figure out how to make marshmallows. There was nothing like roasting a marshmallow over an open fire. The blackened, crispy skin, the mushy center. Heaven. She would experiment in the kitchen and see what she could come up with.

Norbert was bent over a chair he was working on. She smiled to see it looked like her chaise. "Are you making that for Lord Blackford?"

The carpenter turned to her with a smile on his face. "He is very taken with your chair, my lady. I am making one for him and for Wymund as well." The blacksmith's brother pointed to the legs of the chair. "I carved ravens on the wood. Been seeing them around the castle."

The detailed work was exquisite. "They'll love them. You do beautiful work."

The man ducked his head, embarrassed. She pulled the scarf out of her pocket. The wool was a dark brown and would look good against the red of his beard and hair. She handed it to him. Norbert took the scarf, holding it out, a confused look on his face.

"You wrap it around your neck, like this." She took the scarf from him and demonstrated around her neck.

She handed it back to him. He wrapped it around his neck.

"'Tis very comfortable and warm, my lady. I thank you."

Lucy blew a lock of hair out of her face. She'd left it down to keep her neck warm. There was one person who was not getting a scarf for Christmas. You only made gifts for people you liked. If she could give him coal, she would. Clement grated on her nerves. He might have William fooled, but not her. She was convinced he was behind all the near misses.

If she stayed here permanently, she didn't want him living under the same roof. Didn't trust him as far as she could throw him. He snuck around like some of the rats she'd seen in the barn.

One of her men walked toward her. Something wriggled under his cloak.

"One of the cats in the village had kittens. I thought you might like one." He pulled a tiny bundle of fur out of his cloak. The kitten blinked up at her with solid gold eyes. Its coat was beautiful, a dark gray that reminded her of the sea.

The man looked nervous for a moment. "I know some folk fear cats. Cats are good for catching rats and mice. We have a fair number of vermin roaming around."

"Thank you. He's beautiful. Is it a he?"

The man brightened. "'Tis a male, my lady."

Lucy cradled the kitten in her arms. The tiny furry animal promptly stretched out in the crook of her arm and went to sleep. He was absolutely adorable. "I think I shall call him Thor."

The man shook his head. "'Tis a grand name to live up to."

"I think Thor will live up to his name." She carried the kitten into the castle. How quickly did kittens start catching mice? It wasn't like she had a bag of kitten chow she could feed him. She'd have to ask her guard what to feed the kitten. The kitten purred and Lucy felt her heart swell. It seemed she was becoming more and more a part of daily life here in medieval England.

Chapter Twenty-Four

Today was the start of his new life. By now the messenger Clement sent to the king should have reached the court. And when guards arrived to arrest William for treason, it would be too late. Poor Lord Blackford would have fallen over the battlements and met his death. His broken body found on the rocks by his loyal men.

Once Clement had the royal decree granting him Blackford, he would dismiss the men who served under William. Find his own men, loyal to him. And get rid of all the girls. He wanted plump, tasty wenches around the castle.

Clement watched Wymund and a small band of knights ride out of the castle. He waited until he was sure they were far enough away, then made his way to the battlements. "Sound the alarm. Scots at the far gate."

The guard shouted to raise the alarm and pounded down the steps. He could hear the knights shouting as they made their way to the far gate. The door opened and William came running to look out over his land. "Where are the invaders?"

As William searched for the enemy, Clement brought the stone down hard on the back of William's head. He fell with a heavy thud, hitting his head on the stone. Clement hastily tied his hands and feet together and placed a gag around his mouth.

It would take time to sort out the chaos. Clement had paid a band of ruffians to run to and fro, screaming and yelling in the woods at the far western corner of the castle. He could hear the howls of the fake Scots.

Pleased with his deception, Clement pondered how best to kill William. The man was heavy as a horse. If he struggled, Clement wasn't sure he could throw him over the side. He grunted as he propped William up on the bench, his head resting against the wall. He was senseless but would wake soon.

Clement wanted him awake. The man needed to know why Clement hated him so before he killed him. Wanted William to know they were half-brothers and Blackford would now be his. He was pondering whether or not to throw the witch over the edge too. Was Lucy truly a witch? He thought so in the beginning, but she had not performed any feats of magic.

Mayhap she was nothing more than a girl. Clement scratched his backside. He could kill her or he could keep her and bed her. She had a feisty spirit and would likely scream. He liked them to scream when he bedded them. Then he would beat her. Women needed to be beaten daily to keep the demons away. As he was deciding what to do, the door to the battlements opened.

September twenty-third, the first day of fall. Lucy opened the trunk at the foot of the bed and pulled out the ball of rags that used to be her wedding dress. She held it up, looking at the fire through the various rips and tears. At one time, the dress had been beautiful. Snowy white, encrusted with crystals and pearls and ethereal chiffon. Now it wasn't even fit to dust the furniture.

She stripped down to her chemise, and as she was about to pull it over her head, she stopped. If she took off the chemise to put the dress on, she'd be showing way too much skin. But with it on, would the garment hinder her efforts to go home?

Would something from this time period hold her here? She was afraid and yet part of her wanted to stay.

"Get it together. Get your mind right. You have to want to go back with your whole body and soul or it won't work." How was that for a pep talk?

So she pulled the chemise off and pulled the ragged dress on. It would be dark soon, so it wasn't like anyone should notice. The guard on the battlements were used to her acting odd. They'd nod and go back to watching for enemies.

She lifted the blue sparkly shoes out of the trunk and admired them in the light. The wedges were a good four inches high, and she loved the color and the crystals. Lucy buckled them around her ankles and stood, wobbling for a moment. It had been months since she'd worn a heel. For a moment she felt like a little girl playing dress-up.

With a small sniff, she twisted her hair up into a French twist and stuck the pins in to hold the hair. Next came the earrings, necklace and bracelets, which felt cold against her skin.

The trunk closed with a soft thud and she rested her hands on top. Then she straightened her shoulders, stood and wrapped her cloak around her, pulling up the hood. She would take it off on the battlements. With a peek out the door, she blinked. The corridor was empty.

Guess she wouldn't need an excuse to get rid of her guard after all. Where was everyone? She thought she'd heard a commotion earlier but assumed it was the men being men.

Would it hurt when she passed through time again? When she came through, Lucy wasn't sure if lightning struck her or if it was the sensation of traveling through time that hurt so much. She remembered the explosion of color, a sensation of falling and the sound of metal tearing apart. Then nothing.

Her bracelets jangled and she slid them higher on her arm. As she opened the door to the battlements, she thought there was a different guard on duty.

"You. What are you doing here?" Lucy stepped closer and saw Clement standing next to a large bundle. She clapped her hand over her mouth in horror. It was William. He wasn't moving.

She ran over to him. There was blood running down the side of his face. She could see blood in his hair.

"William! William, wake up." She shook him and tried again. "William. You must wake up."

Clement started to laugh. Lucy felt the sting of a slap across her cheek as she turned her ankle in the heels and fell on her butt.

"You are such an ass."

"You will die first, mistress." He laughed. A creepy, insane sound. Clement kicked William. "I don't think he is able to rescue you."

"Let him go."

William stirred, and Clement grabbed his hair, yanking his head back.

"Wake, my lord. You can watch your lady die and then you will follow." William did not move.

Lucy felt sick. How could she help William? In the distance, she heard noise. Shouting. And what looked like torches in the woods.

Clement followed her gaze, a look of satisfaction on his face.

"The guards believe they are fending off an attack from the Scots. There aren't any Scots. I paid a band of ruffians to pretend. This way we will not be interrupted. It wouldn't do for the peasants to see the new Lord Blackford murdering his friend, would it? I will grieve when they find William broken on the rocks. One of the Scots must have made his way through the castle and surprised our lord."

"You are more bonkers than a raccoon swimming in moonshine, you know that, don't you?"

She had to buy time. Soon enough the men would figure out there was no attack. Then they would come back and look for a traitor. He happened to be standing right in front of her.

Clement could see William was coming to, and took care not to get too close, Lucy noted.

William glared at Clement. "What is the meaning of this?"

Lucy inched toward the door, intending to find the guards, but Clement stopped her and pressed a knife to her throat.

He looked at William while he held the knife to her. She could feel the cold point pressing on the flesh.

"When your family fell out of favor with the king, I offered you a place at Blackford."

Clement scoffed. "It is beneath my station for me to take such a position. You still haven't unraveled the plot, have you?" He shook his head. "I am disappointed in you. The lady has addled your mind. The William I knew would have figured out the plot and killed me months ago."

William shook his head as if to dispel the fuzziness. "What cause have you to betray me? We have been friends since childhood. You are like a brother to me."

"I dispatched a messenger to the king. He bears a letter you wrote. To Robert the Bruce. In it you declare your dissatisfaction with our king. You offer an alliance with Scotland. Gold to help in the fight for independence."

Lucy could see the moment Clement's betrayal finally sank in. She knew what it felt like. Wished with all her heart she could help him. Could take the pain away. To know someone you thought of as friend since childhood would betray you so badly, it was a pain she wouldn't wish on anyone.

She didn't know how he could look so calm, but he did. He leaned back against the wall, hands and feet tied. And yet he looked like he was out for a breath of fresh air.

"I ask you again, why betray me?"

"We share the same father."

Talk about dropping a bomb. Lucy couldn't see the resemblance. William looked stunned, while Clement looked smug.

"When my mother died I searched her trunks and found a letter. A letter she wrote to your father. In it, she confessed she was with child. Named him father. Your father was going to declare me his true son. I will show the king the letter. The letter along with proof of your treachery will be enough. The king will award me the gold, the title and Blackford Castle."

Lucy was completely stunned. They were half-brothers. She'd heard William talk of his father with affection. She couldn't imagine what he must be feeling right now. She wanted to go to him, comfort him. But the knife pressed harder and she was afraid if she moved Clement would slit her throat.

"Soon after our father discovered your mother was barren, he looked elsewhere for sons. You know he wanted many sons. Who knows how many bastards there are roaming the countryside. You are naïve, William. You believed him to be a good man. And yet you have no idea he ill-used your mother so. I have known since I was seven years old that we are brothers."

William looked like he was trying to digest the story. And still

Lucy could think of no way to save him.

"Why didn't you tell me?" William looked at his friend with sorrow in his eyes. "Everyone has flaws. Even my father. I would've welcomed you into my life, gladly called you brother."

Clement looked stricken for a moment then recovered. "Lies. You treated me as a servant. Never as a brother."

Inspiration struck. Lucy stomped on her captor's foot as hard as she could with her heel. He yelled out and the knife went flying. She dove for it, sliding across the stone, scraping her arms, but somehow she managed to grab the blade and toss it to William. In an instant Clement was on her, hitting and kicking. It seemed like hours she tried to protect herself, but in reality it was probably only a couple of minutes then he was gone.

William stood there holding a bruised and battered Clement by the throat, anger blazing across his face.

"The only reason I don't run you through is for the affection I held for you these many years. I will not kill you because you are my half-brother. You will live with what you have done. Your punishment is banishment."

William swept Lucy up in his arms, holding her close. He looked over his shoulder at Clement. "Begone in the morning. Never show your face on my lands again. I will kill you the next time I see you."

Chapter Twenty-Five

"Are you unharmed?" William carried her down the stairs to her chamber.

When he'd seen Clement holding a knife to her throat, the bright red blood, William feared his heart would stop.

"You saved me at great risk to yourself. I am in your debt, my brave warrior lady."

She touched the marks on his wrists where he'd tried to loosen the ropes. His half-brother was proficient in tying knots.

His lady put a hand to his cheek and said, so softly he strained to hear, "Why did you let him go?"

In truth, William thought it might not have been one of his best decisions. But he could not kill the only remaining family he had.

He rubbed his eyes. "He grew up envying me and my relationship with our father. I knew his father was a cold man, though I did not know he beat Clement. To grow up wanting something you cannot have. The envy turned his heart black. Filled him with hate."

Thomas entered the chamber. "My lord. My lady. We are not under attack. 'Twas ruffians pretending to be Scots."

Wymund strode in, dirty and tired. "The earl to the west died of fever two months past. The messenger was discovered with his throat slit." The captain of his guard handed him a letter. He recognized the seal. It was his own.

The seal broke with a snap. The handwriting clearly that of Clement. 'Twas as he said. The letter was to Robert the Bruce offering support and gold. William would have been drawn and quartered when the king read this treasonous document.

"I am obliged to you, Wymund." He saw a look pass between the men. "You have heard."

"Why, my lord? Why did you let the traitor go free?" Thomas looked like he was ready to cry or hit something. William sometimes forgot he had not yet seen a score of years.

"Clement and I grew up playing together." He took a breath and looked to Lucy, who smiled at him with love in her eyes. "He is my half-brother. My father and his mother."

Lucy took his hand.

"I did not know until tonight. I thought it better for him to live with the knowledge he will never have what is mine than to kill him. He is banished. If he shows his face on my lands, he will die."

The men nodded and left him alone. William pulled Lucy close. "If he harmed you…"

He kissed her, threading his hands through her glorious hair. The thought of losing her gnawed at his gut. William ran a finger down her soft cheek.

"I love you, Lucy Merriweather."

He looked at her again. She wore the future clothes she'd arrived in. Dread took the place of happiness.

"Were you trying to go back?" He had hoped she would accept

living here. With him.

She kicked off the blue footwear and he caught a glimpse of skin. Seeing his gaze, she blushed and wrapped the cloak around her.

"Today is the first day of fall, I mean autumn. When I came though it was the first day of summer." She looked embarrassed. "I thought I would try one last time." She stood on her tiptoes to kiss his cheek.

"Deep in my heart I didn't really want to go back." She hugged him tight, her face against his chest, muffling her words.

"I love you too, William. When I saw you tied up…my heart stopped."

He spent the rest of the night holding her close. Afraid if he let go she might change her mind and leave him. The fire beckoned as William considered burning the tattered dress and shoes. Lucy seemed to believe she needed them to return to her own time. If he burned them she couldn't leave him…

Cursed knightly vows, he could not, no matter how much he wished. She would have to make the choice to stay with him. Was his love enough?

As Lucy wandered around the village, Thomas and Albin trailing behind her, she wanted to skip and sing. But she knew if she did most of the villagers would think she was even crazier than they suspected.

She was purchasing more wool for crocheting when she heard two women talking. They couldn't see her from where she stood.

For some reason, Lucy hesitated. Later she would wonder what made her do so. As if some part of her knew something wasn't quite right.

"I saw Lord Blackford kissing her. With mine own two eyes," the old woman with the gray dress said.

Her companion, a young woman with black hair down to her waist, made a face. "He will kill her as he did his first wife."

Lucy gasped. Someone took hold of her arm and she jumped.

"Are you unwell, my lady?"

She could see the alarm on Thomas' face. "Come, sit down on the wall."

Lucy let him lead her over to the wall. So many thoughts rushing through her head. What did they mean William killed his first wife? First wife? She didn't know he'd been married.

It was like Simon all over again.

She had to find out what they knew. She sent Albin to fetch her something to drink and waited for the women to walk by. As they made their way toward her, she called out, "Might I have a word?"

The two women looked at her curiously then made their way over to her. "Yes, my lady?" the young one said.

She hesitated then decided it was best to ask straight out. "I didn't mean to overhear you talking, but I did."

Fear filled the women's faces. The old lady spoke up. "We meant no harm, lady."

The young one had an evil look on her face, as if she were enjoying the conversation. "Idle gossip, mistress. Nothing more."

"I would like to know the story. Will you tell me?"

Albin appeared with a tankard of ale and she sent him back to fetch drinks for the women. She gestured to the stone bench.

"Please, sit. And tell me the tale."

Lucy noticed her hands shaking as she took a sip. All the mean things Simon had ever said to her came rushing back. How he always commented on her weight. Her being American. Her Southern accent. And how in the end he'd tried to kill her. All because of her name. Lucy let out a shaky laugh and the women looked at her with fear on their faces.

She knew they probably thought she was unhinged, but she couldn't help it. Was it possible she married William while she was trapped here? Was that why Simon swore her last name was Brandon? And not her sisters?

The boy handed the women cups of ale, turned to her and said, "Anything else, my lady?"

"No. I'm going to rest a bit and talk with these women. I'll be ready to go back soon."

She saw Thomas nearby along with four other men, all keeping an eye on her from a discreet distance.

The two women looked at each other and she guessed they were mother and daughter. The mother started to speak but the younger woman jumped in. She looked like she was in her mid-thirties. Lucy was guessing the woman was probably closer to her own age, if not younger. The woman was pretty but had a hard look to her. She seemed to be happy to tell her the sordid story.

"Lord Blackford killed his wife Georgina. He is a very wealthy man. Some say wealthier than the king. But no one will have him. No one wants to die at his hands. They call him the Butcher of Blackford."

Somehow she managed to sit there while they all finished their drinks. Inside she was ranting and raving. Screaming and shaking. On the outside she knew she looked calm except for the slight trembling of her hands.

She thanked the women and stood up to leave. She started to sway. Thomas caught her under the arm. "Let's get you back to the castle, my lady."

She looked up at him. "Did you know, Thomas?"

He didn't even pretend not to know what she spoke of. "We all know about Lord Blackford's first wife. My lord is a good man. I've never seen him harm a woman. She must have given him cause."

Fear filled her. It shook her to the core to find out William had killed his wife. What was it with her and men? Doubt flooded through her. All her bad decisions scrolling through her head. By the time they got back to the castle, Lucy had made a decision.

She was leaving.

And every day she would keep trying to go home. There had to be another way besides standing on the battlements, right?

And if she couldn't get back, if she were truly trapped here, well, then she'd find work. She could cook, clean, garden. She could crochet. Maybe some other guy with a castle would employ her. She could always build her own shack next to a wall, tend a small garden and hope to survive.

It was better than worrying about being murdered every waking moment.

Chapter Twenty-Six

Lucy packed quickly. She had the dress and apron she was wearing. In the satchel the seamstress had made her, she put the other clothes. She looked longingly at the gorgeous blue velvet dress hanging on a hook and decided to leave it behind. It wasn't like she would need the dress. She was going to have to work for a living. There would be no dancing.

In any other situation she would tell the guy why she was leaving him. But she couldn't take the risk. What if he killed her on the spot? He was the law of the land. He could kill her in broad daylight and no one would blink.

He been nothing but kind to her, given her no indication he meant her harm. But the voice inside her head spoke up. *You thought the same thing about Simon, and look where that got you.*

The voice in her head was right. She had to leave now. How would she escape her guards? Lucy thought for a few moments before opening the door and speaking to the guard on duty.

"Would you have a bath prepared for me?"

They wouldn't notice the sack she was carrying. In the kitchen she could pack food for a few days. She had to get as far away from the castle as she could. Did she dare take a horse?

With a horse she could go further. But she didn't know enough about caring for the animals. She would worry she wasn't doing something right and the animal would suffer. Nope. Lucy had two good legs. It would take longer, but she would walk. Wasn't like she was in a hurry.

Before she left the room, Lucy took the raggedy dress and shoes and stuffed them in the bag as well. She always carried her jewelry and the pins from her hair in the pouch that hung on her waist. Call it superstition or whatever, but she felt like if she had them, she was always ready if an opportunity came up to go back to her own time.

Though after William told her he loved her… Damn. She'd fallen hard for the wrong guy. Again. How could she have been so stupid? Her heart broke all over again. But this time was different. She didn't think she'd survive this loss.

A couple of the women were busy working in the kitchens.

"I'm going to have a bath. Would you prepare me something to eat?"

The kitchen bustled with activity, giving her plenty of time to grab food and stuff it in the sack. One of the new girls brought a tray to the bathing chamber.

"Thank you. I don't need help undressing. You can go."

The girl curtseyed and left. Lucy called out to the man guarding her, "You can stay in the kitchens or go do whatever you want. I plan to be in here for a while."

The man nodded. "I will be in the kitchens if you have need of me, mistress. Thomas does not want us far from you. My lord would disembowel me if anything happened to you."

Lucy seriously hoped not. She didn't want another death on her conscience. Alan's death weighed on her heart. The man who'd saved her from Simon. She couldn't bear another.

The water steamed and smelled like lavender. She decided to go ahead and take a bath. Who knew when she would get another one? As she washed, she tried to figure out where she would go. A large town? Or something small?

She knew traveling alone was a risk, but it couldn't be helped. The men might serve as her personal guard, but they were loyal first and foremost to William.

With a jolt she sat up, water splashing over the side of the wooden tub and onto the stone floor. There was a door in this very room. A door leading down through the secret passages out to the cove.

She could follow the water and make sure no one saw her by staying close to the rocks. Then she would make her way up and around the castle.

Now she had a plan, she didn't want to stay one minute longer. Lucy dried off and dressed as fast as she could. Finished the meal that had been brought to her, made sure everything was packed and, with a sad glance at the closed door, she pressed on the wall, the passage opened and she slipped through.

The cobwebs were gone, the steps scrubbed clean. She kept quiet, listening before moving to make sure no one else was in the passage. Ever since they'd been discovered, the men and boys liked to pop out of the passages unexpectedly.

The smell of salt air reached her as she turned the corner. A weathered door beckoned. Lucy put her hand on the door to open it and someone reached out from the passage to her left, grabbed her and covered her mouth before she could yell for help. The voice next to her ear gave her chills.

"If it isn't the witch."

Lucy's stomach dropped like when you're on a roller coaster and come to the first drop. It was Clement the pig.

"Sneaking away? Not so fast, mistress. I have plans for you." She saw movement and then a shattering pain on the side of her head.

Chapter Twenty-Seven

His protective instincts flared as William kicked the wall of the battlements. "Bloody hell. Where the devil is she?"

He rolled his eyes to the heavens. Why couldn't he have fallen in love with a nice, quiet girl? One who didn't cause the villagers to make the sign of evil every time they saw her. It was getting better, but some still did. He'd seen them do it as she wandered through the village, oblivious.

Thomas cleared his throat. He offered his sword to William. "Kill me, my lord. For I have failed. Mistress Lucy went into the bathing chamber. I had a guard outside the door. He drank too much ale and fell asleep. When he woke, she was gone. He assumed she had gone to her chamber."

The captain of Lucy's guard looked as worried as William felt.

He handed the sword back. "'Tis as much my fault. Her lady's maid said she was going to her chamber to sleep." William cursed again. "I didn't want to disturb her. After dinner I took food to her chamber. It was empty. Her garments are missing." He did not say he'd opened the trunk at the foot of her bed. Searched in vain for her future clothing. She'd left him.

"I will check the wine cellar and stables again, my lord." Thomas backed out of the room looking miserable.

Why would she leave him? Had she planned all along to betray him, like Georgina?

The thought was enough to send him back to battle. There was always a battle raging somewhere. Perchance he could fight until he could forget her enchanting gray eyes.

William snorted. Not bloody likely. She was a part of him. Some days he felt he couldn't breathe until he'd seen her. He was like a young boy following around the woman he wanted to woo. Had she finally found a way to go back to her future? The thought struck terror into his heart. He slumped down in her chair in front of the fire, staring unseeing into the flames.

Lucy came to cold and shivering. The room she was in was dark. Quiet. She could feel rough stone walls. Was she in one of the unfinished buildings, or maybe one of the towers that hadn't been repaired yet?

A candle cast a small circle of light. "I see you are awake."

"You," she spat. "William will kill you when he sees you. He banished you."

Clement knelt down beside her close enough she could see the madness in his eyes. No one knew where she had gone. When they found her room empty and her clothes missing, they would assume she'd run away.

Would William search for her? Or would he move on to his next victim?

Her captor handed her a hard piece of bread and wooden cup filled with wine. "'Tis all you get."

"Are you going to untie me so I can eat?"

He looked at her a long moment and fear sliced through her heart.

"I cannot decide whether to kill you or bed you."

Oh hell no. She opened her mouth and screamed for all she was worth.

Clement chuckled. "Go ahead. Scream as loud and as long as you like. No one will hear you." He smirked. "And if they do, they will think there are ghosts at Blackford."

He untied her hands and tied the rope to a ring in the wall. She shifted to loosen the bonds around her waist.

"Eat." He stood next to a corner of the wall. When he pushed on it, the wall swung open and Lucy realized she was in a tiny room in one of the secret passages.

"The door bars from the outside. No one will find you. They haven't explored these passages. They don't connect to the others."

He started to leave and terror filled her. "How long are you going to leave me here?"

"Long enough."

With that, the door swung closed and she heard the bar slide into place. She would not let her fear of being left here to die overwhelm her. First things first. Lucy ate the gritty bread, drank the wine then stood and explored the tiny room as best she could, given the length of the rope. The crazy man was great with knots. She gave up trying to untie them. When she tried to push on the door where she'd seen him go through the passage, it wouldn't budge. She was trapped and at the mercy of a total lunatic.

Lucy found both her satchels in the darkness, grateful Clement had thrown the bags in with her. She opened up one bag and ate some of the cheese she'd put in for her escape. Then she used the satchel containing her clothes to rest her head on. With her cloak wrapped tight around her, she tried to sleep.

Were there rats in here? Lucy listened. The only sound was her heavy breathing. Thank the stars there weren't rats. Things always looked better in the morning. Maybe then she'd come up with a plan.

Lucy woke sometime later not knowing where she was. She'd slept fitfully, with visions of all kinds of gruesome deaths Clement might have planned for her.

Even if she escaped him, then what? She had no means. A tiny bit of food. But no money or transportation. And given her abysmal sense of direction, she most likely would end up in Scotland and be burned at the stake. Based on the people she'd met so far, she didn't think anyone would help her. They'd either know she came from the castle or think she was strange and turn away from her.

Lucy would have to find a way to rescue herself. And then she would have to figure out what came next. One thing she knew? She wouldn't put herself in danger by staying with William. Somehow she had to find a way back home.

William didn't get any sleep that night. His men swore they heard screaming in the walls. Some of the young girls working in the castle said it was haunted. And many of the smaller boys believed them. It was enough to make him want to leave. Find the first battle he could and lose himself in the fight.

William and his men searched the passages throughout the day. They found no trace of Lucy. It was as if she had disappeared. Had she found her way back?

It had to be the only reason she wouldn't tell him she was leaving. Two days she'd been missing and he knew he would find no sleep tonight. He paced in front of the fire in the hall.

"I do not believe the lady has come to harm."

Wymund sat down in a chair in front of the fire and William reluctantly sat down across from him waiting.

His captain looked weary.

"Tell me," William demanded.

"When she was in the village, she heard talk."

Dread coursed through his body.

"Thomas found the two women she was seen having speech with. They told her you murdered Georgina."

William cursed. She wasn't hurt. Lucy had left him. After she'd told him how Simon betrayed her, it would've been her first instinct to run far and fast. She would be all alone. Unfamiliar with the lands around her. He leapt to his feet.

"Send the men out. We need to find her before harm befalls her." He started for the door but Wymund stopped him with a hand on his arm.

"William, 'tis the middle of the night. The men will search for her in the morning."

His captain placed a hand on William's shoulder. "We will find her. She won't have gone far. She has a terrible sense of direction." He smiled, and William felt the tiniest bit better.

He would find her and then he would tell her the truth about Georgina. Hope she would forgive him. If she did, he would drop to his knees and beg her to marry him.

Chapter Twenty-Eight

Two long days. Lucy was beginning to wonder if she would be trapped in this tiny room forever. She shuddered thinking of Clement leaving her and letting her starve slowly to death. What a horrible way to die.

The man took great pleasure in detailing all the ways he was going to kill her. All of them involved William being present. So she would see him one last time before she died. And she laughed to herself. Clement would kill her instead of William. Did it really matter which one ended her life?

She thought she was losing her grip on reality. The door opened and her captor sauntered in. At least, she assumed it was him. The candle gave off a pitiful amount of light. But then she sniffed and smelled him from across the tiny room.

"It's time."

She tried to make a run for it, but he knocked her to the ground and she felt her cheek scrape against the stone. He tied her arms behind her and yanked her up by her hair.

He marched her out of the tiny passage through a narrow passageway and up several flights of stairs. When the door opened, she blinked at the moonlight. After being in darkness, it seemed unnaturally bright.

She was on the roof of one of the towers. She opened her mouth to scream, but the sound was cut off as he anticipated what she would do and tightly tied a gag around her mouth.

There was a huge cistern on the roof. He saw her looking at it and grinned.

"The water collects here and is carried to the lower floors through pipes. That's how the cold water comes out in the chambers."

He sneered at her. "The castle was built on the site of an old Roman fort. I would wager you have nothing as fine where you come from."

She stared back at him, furiously trying to come up with a plan that didn't involve throwing herself over the battlements to her death.

The cistern was rectangular in shape, and if she had known it was there before, she would've thought it was some kind of medieval swimming pool. She shuddered thinking how cold the water would be.

"Death by drowning is a suitable end for one like you. I had William well in hand. He would have been content to let me run the castle while he went back to warring. In time I would have poisoned him, gained favor with the king and been rich. Then you showed up and ruined everything."

He pulled her closer to the low stone lip of the pool. It didn't look deep, but considering she was tied, he could easily drown her by sitting on her.

Lucy tried to scream again, but all that came out were muffled sounds. If only someone would see her up here.

"I saw him watching you. Knew he would make you the next lady of Blackford. So I plotted to have him tried for treason. You thwarted my plans. At every turn you have caused me a great deal of effort and trouble."

He pulled out a knife and put it to her throat. "Step on my foot and I'll gut you like a pig." He jerked her hair hard and she nodded. "I'm going to remove the gag. Scream and I'll slit your throat where you stand."

She gave another jerky nod. When the gag fell away, Lucy licked her chapped lips. Panic threatened to overwhelm her. *Hold it together. No one will find you. You have to save yourself.*

"Bless your heart. You can try drowning me, but I thought you knew...witches can't drown." There. See if that statement would buy her some time.

He looked at her in horror then pressed the knife harder against her throat. She felt a prick like a needle and a warm trickle.

"If you are a witch then turn into a bird and fly away."

The rectangular pool took up most of the floor space on the tower roof. There was a small area between the lip of the pool and the wall, which ended at the back of her knees. She leaned against the low wall, trying to dislodge stone, and heard a few pebbles fall. If only someone heard and investigated, she would be saved.

She had to buy time. "I will not turn into a bird and fly away until I punish you first for your disrespect."

He made the sign of the cross at her with his free hand. As she pulled away, he grabbed her hair and yanked her close, the knife nicking her collarbone.

 Lucy decided it was now or never. Either he would slit her throat and she would die quickly or he would drown her and it would be slow. No matter what, she knew she was going to die.

A sense of quiet and clarity settled over her. She took a deep breath and screamed with all she had. He cut her, and she leaned in and bit his ear as hard as she could, gagging when she tasted blood. Clement yelped and dropped the knife, and it clattered over the edge. Lucy screamed again as he lunged for her. For the first time in her life, she wished she had short hair.

They fell into the water with a splash. She struggled to get up as he pushed her under with both hands and sat on her. Damn, he was heavy.

Lucy saw the moonlight from under the water, could see Clement above her, his hands pressing down on her chest as Lucy kicked and thrashed, cursing the heavy dress. The garment weighed her down. He was so heavy she couldn't get him off.

Her lungs ready to burst, she heard a sound muffled by the water. A sound like a cry. A black shape hurtled toward Clement's head.

He threw up his hands screaming and Lucy sat up with a gasp, greedily sucking in air.

A raven attacked him. The bird flew at his face, raking him with its talons and pecking him.

She gathered up her sodden dress as best she could and started to run. Adrenaline gave her the energy she needed to focus. Lucy ran blindly down the stairs through the passages, stumbling, searching for a way out.

She came to a passageway where she could hear the ocean. It seemed to be a long corridor. At the end, she entered another door, ran up the steps and heard voices.

Lucy screamed and screamed as she went up the stairs. Men were shouting and she swore she heard one man say there was a ghost. It was almost as if she could only reach through the wall separating them, she could reach the men.

She kept climbing the stairs, fear giving her strength as she heard a scrabbling behind her.

"Witch. Sending your familiar after me. I will kill you." Lucy looked over her shoulder to see Clement. His face bloody and one eye missing. He was almost to her. She reached for the door, flung it open and sighed in relief. She was on the battlements she knew so well. There would be guards here.

An awful smell filled her nose, and Lucy knew he was almost to her. Where were the guards?

As she leaned over the wall to look for anyone, Clement grabbed hold of her dress and spun her around. She felt a sharp pain and fell against the stone. As she sank down on the bench, time seemed to still. The sound of Clement screaming, the sound of the ocean…all faded.

A violent shuddering racked her body. It seemed to start in her feet and travel up through her spine. Lucy felt like she were the beaters of a mixer clacking together. Turning round and round. Tiny whimpers escaped. She couldn't stop shaking, couldn't control her body.

As if from a great distance she saw William running toward her, a look of fear on his face. Everything started to fade, melting into a watercolor painting. And then it was as if she were watching two movies at once.

She could see William and the men. See William and Clement fighting. But she also saw what looked like electric lights. And what she swore were cars in the distance.

And in that moment Lucy knew she could make the choice. Knew why she couldn't go back all the other times she'd tried.

It wasn't his blood staining the stone by the bench. It was hers. And now her blood was on the stone, she could go home.

Lucy reached out with both hands.

Chapter Twenty-Nine

William heard the call of the raven and looked upward toward the sound. The bird was flying around the battlements. And as he searched he spied a figure. By the saints, 'twas Lucy.

He'd sent the guards out to search for her, so there was no one on the battlements to save her. They'd searched and searched and found no trace, and now he knew why. There was another set of secret passages. How many bloody secret passages could one castle contain?

Clement had used the passages to come and go without being seen, probably since William banished him. Cold fury filled him as he took the steps to the roof two at a time. As his foot touched the last step, he reached out, as if he could cross the distance and stop the blade.

Lucy fell back against the stone with the cry of a wounded animal. William's mind went blank; the only command urging him onward was to save his beloved. He tucked, rolled and came to his feet, knees bent and perfectly balanced with sword in one hand.

In the time it took him to draw breath, his sword arm flashed down and ran his half-brother through. As Clement died in his arms, he looked up, eyes full of disbelief. "Well done, brother, you killed me first." Then he slumped in William's embrace, silent forever.

William was beyond sadness. An emptiness filled him as he let go of Clement's body. He turned to aid Lucy.

"Nay! Do not go!" She started to fade in front of his eyes.

The raven cawed and landed on the stone wall near Lucy, and William felt the hair on his arms stand. There was something strange about the bird. Something otherworldly.

William could almost see through Lucy. He had a moment when he thought he should let her go back to her own time. To learn the fates of her sisters. Make a new life in an easier time.

But the selfish part of him, the part that loved her, and would lay down his life for her gladly, bellowed deep within him like a mad beast.

William reached out.

His hand went through her. A calm he experienced in battle fell over him. William ignored the terrible cold and reached with both hands until he touched warm flesh.

"She is mine! You cannot have her!" With a great cry, he pulled with all his might. A cold pierced his bones, held his heart in its grip, and he knew he was stealing her back from the future.

As he held her in his arms, waiting for her to come to her senses, he prayed she would not despise him for the rest of her life. For he had stolen her from time itself. A voice whispered on the air that it was her only choice. She would not have another. Lucy now belonged here in his time. The overlarge black bird called out as it flew off into the moonlight.

Lucy had had it up to here with fainting and waking up in strange places. She opened her eyes a fraction. She was no longer in the tiny, dark room. The faint smell of horse and male made her nose twitch. Soft, worn linen under her fingers. She was in her own bed. In a chair next to her, William slumped, eyes closed.

The movement woke him. He knelt beside the bed.

"In truth, I watched you fade." He took her hands in his and held them so tightly she heard the bones crack.

"Can you ever forgive me? I kept you from going home."

She saw the agony in his eyes. The love he felt for her. Certainty filled her heart. She loved him, but—

Lucy took a deep breath. "Did you kill your wife?"

She waited for him to answer, trying to decide what she would do if he said yes. The doorway between here and the future was closed. When she'd been in the middle of the cold and saw both worlds, she knew this was her one chance. He'd pulled her back from her own time.

So if he said he killed his wife? She could think about scenarios all day and night, but in the end she couldn't know how she would react until he answered.

William made a noise in the back of his throat. "I was married once. Georgina was very beautiful." He looked at Lucy with love in his eyes.

"But she was not beautiful on the inside. She was cruel and treated everyone she met with scorn. Our marriage was not a happy one. I was away fighting most of the time. She married me for my wealth and reputation on the battlefield. Even then I had attained great wealth tourneying and fighting throughout the lands."

He paused as if he needed time to breathe. To fortify himself. Clear green eyes bored into her, and she could count the tiny gold flecks within them.

"I did not murder her. Georgina had a lover. A man she met in the village. He was poor and she found him a position on our small estate. They concocted a plan. She would fake her death and run away with him."

She sat still listening to him, afraid to move until the story was done. William worked a knot out of her hair.

"I knew she wasn't dead. The woman should have left her clothing and jewels behind if she wanted me to believe she was dead. Her maid sobbed out the tale. She helped Georgina pack, saw her off in a carriage. The poor girl died of a fever a few weeks later, so she could not clear my name. By the time I caught up with Georgina, the fever had taken her. Her lover was desolate and took his own life in grief. I found them together."

The only sound in the room was the crackling of the fire.

Lucy's heart soared. She was wrong. William was nothing like Simon. He was different. With him she could truly be herself. And isn't that what we all really want in life? Someone we can be ourselves with. Instead of believing true love existed, she'd let her fear rule her life for so many years. Anything to avoid the risk of opening up to another person and getting hurt in return. What an idiot she'd been. True love did exist, even if she had to fall over seven hundred years through time to find the man meant for her.

"I believe you. I'm sorry you have had to live with people thinking you murdered your wife." She pulled him close, and he climbed onto the bed next to her.

"When I was...fading, I could see you in front of me. And at the same time, I could see my own time. I knew I had a choice to make—I could choose which life I wanted. My heart had already made the decision when I reached out for you. You took hold of me at the same time, and I think that's why I stayed."

William slid off the bed and went down on one knee. He reached into the pouch at his waist and held up a ring. "I will give you all that I possess. I will love you until the end of your days. Know that I will spend every day of my life making you happy."

She gasped. The band was gold and inset with an emerald as big as her thumb. He slid it on her finger, where it fit perfectly.

Underneath his grumbles and rough edges was a good man. She would take a knight in tarnished armor any day.

"Will you marry me, Lucy Merriweather?"

Her hand trembled as she looked at the ring. It felt right on her finger, warm and comforting.

"When you truly love someone, you listen and accept them for who they are, past and all. I should have come to you after those women told me the story. Instead I ran. I let the fear I felt over what I had been through in the past cloud my judgment."

Her voice broke. "I'm so sorry. In the future when you make me mad, and I know you will"—Lucy wiped away tears of happiness—"I will come to you and we will talk. You are not your past. I am not my past. Together we will build a future."

He gathered her in his arms, his voice rough. "I will love you through this life to the next. I will love you for centuries so somehow you will know to come back to me."

A single tear fell. "Every choice I made led me to you."

The love she felt for William washed over her. "My future is here. In the past with you." Lucy said a prayer for her family. She had mourned them enough and it was time to let go. She would never forget them, would always love them.

And then she heard the raven. Whom she had come to think of as her own special bird. A thought made her smile. She would write a letter and find someplace safe to put it in the castle. Maybe, just maybe, if her sisters weren't dead...they would come looking for her. Find the letter. And know that she was happy. She had found her happily ever after.

Chapter Thirty

Six Months Later

Lucy was almost certain, but now she knew for sure. The only thing to make finding out more perfect? If her family were here to hear the news. William entered their chamber, swept her into his arms and kissed her soundly.

"You're looking well today, wife."

She beamed at him. William hesitated for a moment, clearly realizing he was supposed to notice something. "Did you perchance make a new dessert for me?" The man had turned into a total sugar hound.

"No. Something better," she said.

"Better than dessert?" William looked dubious.

Lucy took his hand and placed it on her stomach over the slight bulge.

"You're going to be a father," she told him, her eyes full of love for her husband.

William looked shell-shocked. He stood there with his mouth opening and closing, breathing through his mouth.

"By the saints." Then he picked her up and carried her to the bed. "You should rest. If it's a girl, we shall name her after one of your sisters."

Lucy felt tears of happiness run down her face. "And if it's a boy, should we name him after your father?"

William's happiness dimmed. "Not after what he did to my mother. His infidelity broke her heart. If it's a boy, we will name him after your father. Would you like that?"

"Very much. And when we have the next one… If it's a girl, I'd like to name her after your mother."

William looked pale. Then recovered with a brilliant smile. "Let's fill the hall full of children. Wait until I tell the men. Wymund will have the babes fighting in the lists before they can walk."

"Even the girls?"

William grinned at her. "Even the girls. 'Tis good for a girl to know how to take care of herself. Though she'll always have the men watching over her."

 Her husband pulled her close and they stood there in the room content. A fire crackled in the hearth while snow fell outside. Life was perfect.

Lucy had found her very own knight. In slightly tarnished armor. She kissed her husband.

Fairy tales do come true. Happily ever after exists, but only if you're willing to fight for it.

Chapter Thirty-One

Present Day - Holden Beach, North Carolina

Melinda Merriweather slammed the laptop shut so hard the table wobbled. "Have you seen the story?" Without waiting for her sister's answer, Melinda ranted, "It says—and I quote—*Simon Grey, Lord Blackford, and his American guest, Lucy Merriweather, were lost at sea after a crumbling wall at Blackford Castle gave way and they plunged to their deaths. The treacherous currents swept the bodies out to sea.*"

She arched a brow at her youngest sister, the anger stretching her face tight. "What a load of horseshit. We are going back."

"No. I can't deal with seeing that desolate place again." Charlotte shivered. "That place oozes sadness and heartbreak."

She pushed her chair back and stood to look out at the ocean. "She's gone, sweetie. We have to accept it." Charlotte put a hand on the glass. "I can't stay here. Everything reminds me of Lucy."

Melinda didn't want to hear the rest, but Charlotte hurried on as if she knew. "So I'm leaving. But I'm not going to England. I need to get away. Far away. There's a gig in Djibouti and I'm taking it. I leave tomorrow."

How could Charlotte not want to go back? There had to be something the authorities had missed. They'd flown over as soon as they were contacted about Lucy. At that time, Melinda and her sister had been so distraught she couldn't think straight. Poor Aunt Pittypat died of a heart attack the same day Lucy went missing.

The cops found Lucy's phone smashed on the rocks. But her purse was in the small cottage on the property, along with all her clothes. Melinda didn't think her sister would leave her purse and passport unattended. The facts made sense, yet something felt off.

A feeling was enough. Melinda was going back to England and not leaving until the feelings of wrongness went away. Lucy would've done the same for her.

Melinda opened up the laptop again and started to make plans.

Books by Cynthia Luhrs

Listed in the correct reading order

THRILLERS
There Was A Little Girl
When She Was Good

TIME TRAVEL SERIES
A Knight to Remember
Knight Moves
Lonely is the Knight
Merriweather Sisters Medieval Time Travel Romance
Boxed Set Books 1-3
Darkest Knight
Forever Knight
First Knight
Thornton Brothers Medieval Time Travel Romance
Boxed Set Books 1-3
Last Knight

COMING 2017 - 2018
Beyond Time
Falling Through Time
Lost in Time

My One and Only Knight
A Moonlit Knight
A Knight in Tarnished Armor

THE SHADOW WALKER GHOST SERIES
Lost in Shadow
Desired by Shadow
Iced in Shadow
Reborn in Shadow
Born in Shadow
Embraced by Shadow
The Shadow Walkers Books 1-3
The Shadow Walkers Books 4-6
Entire Shadow Walkers Boxed Set Books 1-6

A JIG THE PIG ADVENTURE
(Children's Picture Books)
Beware the Woods
I am NOT a Chicken!

August 2016 – December 2017 My Favorite Things
Journal & Coloring Book for Book Lovers

Want More?

Thank you for reading my book. Reviews help other readers find books. I welcome all reviews, whether positive or negative and love to hear from my readers. To find out when there's a new book release, please visit my website http://cluhrs.com/ and sign up for my newsletter. Please like my page on Facebook. http://www.facebook.com/cynthialuhrsauthor
Without you dear readers, none of this would be possible.

P.S. Prefer another form of social media? You'll find links to all my social media sites on my website.

Thank you!

About the Author

Cynthia Luhrs writes time travel because she hasn't found a way (yet) to transport herself to medieval England where she's certain a knight in slightly tarnished armor is waiting for her arrival. She traveled a great deal and now resides in the colonies with three tiger cats who like to disrupt her writing by sitting on the keyboard. She is overly fond of shoes, sloths, and tea.

Also by Cynthia: There Was a Little Girl and the Shadow Walker Ghost Series.